Small Change

Vermillion tossed the coin high into the air.

Clint drew and fired. The coin jumped even higher as his bullet struck. As the coin started to fall, he fired again and the coin jumped again.

The coin fell to the ground, and Vermillion picked it up.

"One hole," he said.

"Ha!" someone shouted. "A hit and a miss!"

Clint took the coin, looked at it, then handed it back.

"Look closer," Clint said.

Kit came over and took the coin. Ed Cory walked over, followed by Cole Weston.

"This hole is not round," Kit said. "It's oblong. See?"

She handed the coin to Cory.

"I'll be damned," he said. "He did it twice. Dead through the middle . . . twice!"

DON'T MISS THESE
ALL-ACTION WESTERN SERIES
FROM THE BERKLEY PUBLISHING GROUP

THE GUNSMITH by J. R. Roberts

Clint Adams was a legend among lawmen, outlaws, and ladies. They called him . . . the Gunsmith.

LONGARM by Tabor Evans

The popular long-running series about Deputy U.S. Marshal Custis Long—his life, his loves, his fight for justice.

SLOCUM by Jake Logan

Today's longest-running action Western. John Slocum rides a deadly trail of hot blood and cold steel.

BUSHWHACKERS by B. J. Lanagan

An action-packed series by the creators of Longarm! The rousing adventures of the most brutal gang of cutthroats ever assembled—Quantrill's Raiders.

DIAMONDBACK by Guy Brewer

Dex Yancey is Diamondback, a Southern gentleman turned con man when his brother cheats him out of the family fortune. Ladies love him. Gamblers hate him. But nobody pulls one over on Dex . . .

WILDGUN by Jack Hanson

The blazing adventures of mountain man Will Barlow—from the creators of Longarm!

TEXAS TRACKER by Tom Calhoun

J. T. Law: the most relentless—and dangerous—manhunter in all Texas. Where sheriffs and posses fail, he's the best man to bring in the most vicious outlaws—for a price.

THE GUNSMITH

322

LOUISIANA SHOOT-OUT

J. R. ROBERTS

JOVE BOOKS, NEW YORK

THE BERKLEY PUBLISHING GROUP
Published by the Penguin Group
Penguin Group (USA) Inc.
375 Hudson Street, New York, New York 10014, USA
Penguin Group (Canada), 90 Eglinton Avenue East, Suite 700, Toronto, Ontario M4P 2Y3, Canada
(a division of Pearson Penguin Canada Inc.)
Penguin Books Ltd., 80 Strand, London WC2R 0RL, England
Penguin Group Ireland, 25 St. Stephen's Green, Dublin 2, Ireland (a division of Penguin Books Ltd.)
Penguin Group (Australia), 250 Camberwell Road, Camberwell, Victoria 3124, Australia
(a division of Pearson Australia Group Pty. Ltd.)
Penguin Books India Pvt. Ltd., 11 Community Centre, Panchsheel Park, New Delhi—110 017, India
Penguin Group (NZ), 67 Apollo Drive, Rosedale, North Shore 0632, New Zealand
(a division of Pearson New Zealand Ltd.)
Penguin Books (South Africa) (Pty.) Ltd., 24 Sturdee Avenue, Rosebank, Johannesburg 2196,
South Africa

Penguin Books Ltd., Registered Offices: 80 Strand, London WC2R 0RL, England

This is a work of fiction. Names, characters, places, and incidents either are the product of the author's imagination or are used fictitiously, and any resemblance to actual persons, living or dead, business establishments, events, or locales is entirely coincidental.

LOUISIANA SHOOT-OUT

A Jove Book / published by arrangement with the author

PRINTING HISTORY
Jove edition / October 2008

Copyright © 2008 by Robert J. Randisi.
Cover illustration by Sergio Giovine.

ISBN: 978-0-515-14541-0

JOVE®
Jove Books are published by The Berkley Publishing Group,
a division of Penguin Group (USA) Inc.,
375 Hudson Street, New York, New York 10014.
JOVE is a registered trademark of Penguin Group (USA) Inc.
The "J" design is a trademark belonging to Penguin Group (USA) Inc.

PRINTED IN THE UNITED STATES OF AMERICA

10 9 8 7 6 5 4 3 2 1

ONE

Clint Adams liked New Orleans because it was like no other city in the country. In fact, it seemed like a city that had been plucked from another country and dropped into the southern United States.

The different sections of the city held their own appeal. The Garden District, Metairie, Magazine Street—they all offered unique opportunities for a visitor to enjoy themselves. But Clint's preference had always been the French Quarter.

The Quarter—or *Vieux Carré* as the locals referred to it—the oldest and most famous neighborhood in New Orleans, boasted and maintained a distinctive European flavor. Part of the reason for that was the fact that most of the French Quarter buildings were erected during the Spanish rule over the area. Once distinctly French, the area's architecture changed when, after a great fire in 1794, the Spanish were left to rebuild.

Clint favored the hotels along Bourbon Street and checked himself into one with wrought-iron galleries overlooking the street. (The difference between "galleries" and "balconies" was that a gallery had iron poles supporting it from underneath while a balcony was attached to the side of the building.)

Since his hotel bill was being taken care of by the organizer of the Louisiana Shoot-out, he picked one of the best ones and requested one of the best rooms. He did this without guilt because when Cole Weston first came to him in Labyrinth, his offer was hard to resist—even though Clint tried to, at first . . .

"Fella named Weston is out front askin' for you," Rick Hartman said to Clint.

Clint looked around the table that was located in a private room in back of Rick's Place. The other four cardplayers stared at him.

"Can he wait?" Clint asked.

"I don't know," Rick said. "I don't know what he wants." He leaned over and lowered his voice, as if he were speaking into Clint's ear, but the others could all hear him. "I'm not your social secretary."

Clint smiled.

"Okay, let me finish this hand and I'll come out."

"I'll tell him."

Rick left the room. Clint looked down at the full house in his hand—he'd drawn two aces to go with the three jacks that had been dealt to him—and said, "A hundred."

Clint promised the other players he'd be back and, in fact, left his chips on the table to reinforce the promise. None of them wanted their money to walk out the door with him.

He walked out into the saloon, saw Rick standing at the bar with a tall man in his forties. Right off he noticed the pair of pearl-handled Colts the man was wearing. Men with guns like that either couldn't use them at all and wore them for show, or they were very good with them.

"Mr. Weston?" Clint said, approaching the men.

Weston straightened from leaning on the bar and stared at Clint. He'd been wrong about the man's age. He looked old, but he was probably only mid-thirties. He stared at Clint with unabashed admiration.

"Clint Adams!"

"That's right."

"I'll let you two talk," Rick said. "Beers are on the house."

"Thanks, Rick."

"Thank you, Mr. Hartman," Weston said.

As Rick walked away, Clint signaled the bartender to bring him a beer.

"What can I do for you, Mr. Weston?" he asked, accepting the cold mug. "Can we talk here or would you prefer to sit?"

"Actually, I'd like to sit."

"Right over here."

It was midday, so there were plenty of tables available at Rick's. Clint led Weston to an empty one in the back.

Clint sat so he could see the door, Weston with his back to it.

"I've heard a lot about this place," the man said.

"Really? From who?"

"I've, uh, read some of the books about you. They mention this place."

"They do?"

Weston nodded.

Clint was going to have to think about that. After all these years he'd hate to have to give up Rick's, and Labyrinth, but if the dime novels were giving it away as someplace people could find him . . .

"That's how I knew where to come lookin' for you," Weston said, as if confirming Clint's thoughts.

"I'm a little busy at the moment, Mr. Weston, so if you could get to the point?"

"Oh, sure," Weston said. "The point is simple. We're holdin' a shoot-out and we'd like you to come and participate."

TWO

"Let me get this straight," Clint said. "You want me to participate in a shoot-out?"

"Okay," Weston said, "I'm afraid I put that wrong. See, we're holding a sharpshooting contest in Louisiana. And we're callin' it the Louisiana Shoot-out."

"Look, I don't participate in sharpshooting contests or exhibitions—"

"Oh, this is most definitely a competition," Weston said.

"Well, I don't compete with my gun—"

"Oh, no," Weston said, "no, no, no, you misunderstand. I haven't been sent here to invite you to compete. No, no, we know that you would most probably win. No, we would like you to be one of the judges."

"A judge?"

"Yes," Weston said. "We'll put you up in the hotel of your choice, cover all your meals and expenses."

"And where in Louisiana is the competition being held?"

"New Orleans," Weston said, "on the grounds of the Fairground Racetrack. Do you know the racetrack?"

"Know it, and have enjoyed it. I also love the French Quarter."

"Then you'll do it?"

"No."

Weston sat back in his chair as if he'd been slapped.

"But . . . why not?"

"I don't like contests," Clint said, "especially when they involve guns."

"Why?"

"Leads to trouble."

"Oh, not this time," Weston said.

"Why not?"

"We're going to be very careful," Weston said. "We'll have very good security."

"Really?"

"Yes," Weston said, "we're askin' Heck Thomas if he'll supervise security."

Clint laughed.

"Heck won't do it."

"Why not?"

"He likes this sort of thing almost as much as I do," Clint said.

"Of course," Weston said. "You and he are friends?"

"We are."

"Wouldn't it be good to see each other?"

"We do, occasionally. That's not a selling point with either one of us. Have you approached Heck yet?"

"No," he said, "someone else is doin' that. Mr. Adams—"

"Clint."

"Clint," Weston said, "there'll be racing, gambling, shooting, the French Quarter and all it has to offer. And all your expenses will be covered."

"If I do this," Clint said, "I'd want to go top-of-the-line. Can you handle that?"

"We have the backing of several wealthy men," Weston said. "Money is not a problem."

New Orleans at somebody else's expense. Now that was a selling point . . .

"When is this shoot-out supposed to take place?"

"Next month."

"And last how long?"

"Five days."

Clint leaned back, tilted his head to the right, and looked at Weston's revolvers.

"You any good with those?"

Weston looked down at them.

"Yes."

"Will you be competing?"

"I will."

Clint sipped his beer and thought about it. He had nothing planned for next month, and some rest and relaxation in New Orleans sounded good.

"You covering my expenses," Clint asked, "or giving me expense money?"

"Whichever way you want to do it, Clint," Weston said. "Will you do it?"

"How many competitors?" Clint asked, to give himself more time to think.

"I'm not sure," Weston said. "We're still gettin' people signin' up."

"A lot of them?"

"Oh, yes," Weston said. "A lot of 'em. This is gonna be a big event—even bigger if we can announce you as one of our judges."

"Who are the others?"

"Still recruitin'," Weston said. "We're hopin' to get a few more people like you with reputations. I mean, not that there's anybody else like you, but—"

"I know what you mean, Weston," he said.

"Call me Cole."

"Okay, Cole."

They sat in silence for a few seconds and then Weston asked, "Okay . . . what?"

"Okay, I'll do it."

THREE

Clint didn't usually travel with luggage, but this time he brought a carpetbag with him, along with his saddle-bags. He dropped them on the bed in his hotel room and then walked to the window to gaze down on Bourbon Street. Actually the windows were French doors that opened out onto a wrought-iron gallery. He walked to the railing and looked down.

He loved the pulse of this place, the decadence of it, but he would never choose to live here. For one thing, it was actually below sea level. He'd heard of times when the city flooded and the bodies of the dead floated down the street from the cemeteries.

For another thing, the city didn't always smell good. Some times better, some times worse than others. Summers were bad, but this was fall. Today it smelled just fine to him.

There was a knock on the door then. He turned away from the street and reentered the room. As always he answered the door with his gun in his hand.

"Sir," a man said, "we neglected to give you this note when you checked in. My apologies."

"And you are?"

"The manager, sir," the man said. "Of course you understand that your accommodations have been taken care of?"

Clint studied the man. Well dressed, mid-forties, about five and a half feet tall but very comfortable with who he was.

"Yes, I understand."

"Very good, sir," the man said. "My name is Tate. Please ask for anything you want."

"Thank you, Mr. Tate."

The man, in the act of turning away, stopped and said, "Just Tate, sir."

"All right . . . Tate."

The manager nodded and walked away. Clint closed the door and opened the note.

It was from Cole Weston: *"Sorry I couldn't be there to meet you. If you get in early come out to the Fairgrounds and take a look. Then we'll have some Cajun supper."*

Clint liked Cajun food. He also wanted to see what was going on at the Fairgrounds. If he had some time, he wanted to take in some of the races, as well.

He left his carpetbag packed and on his bed and left the room.

The Fairgrounds were alive with activity. Horse racing was going on—and, in fact, a race was being run at the moment Clint arrived. He left that for later, though, and walked toward all the commotion that was going on away from the races.

There were several tables set up for competitors to sign in. Across the field he could see targets being set up. Also in the area were some drummers erecting booths to conduct business in, and at least one medicine wagon.

"As I live and breathe," a voice said.

Clint turned and saw Heck Thomas walking toward him. Thomas had made his reputation as a lawman, a railroad detective, and a private detective. Now it appeared he was going to be head of security for the Louisiana Shoot-out.

Thomas approached with his hand out and Clint grasped it.

"How're you doin', Heck?" he asked.

"I'm doin' fine," the other man said. "I told them they wouldn't get you to do this."

"Well, if it was happening anywhere else, probably not, but I happen to like Cajun food."

"And Cajun women?"

"They're both hot and spicy."

"That they are."

"How did they convince you to do this?"

"I wasn't doin' anythin' else," he said, "and they're payin' me well."

"Anybody else here?" By that Clint meant, anyone else they both knew.

"I ain't seen anyone," Heck said, "but today's the first day I'm walkin' around here."

"You got other men working security?"

"Three," he said, "and I picked 'em."

"Anybody I know?"

"No," Heck said. "Young fellas, but pretty good ones. They can handle a gun and they can take orders."

"Sounds good. Have you met any other judges?"

"No."

"Seen Cole Weston around?"

"Who?"

"A fella wearing a pair of pearl-handled Colts."

"Oh, him," Heck said. "Yeah, he's been around. He any good with those, or are they for show?"

"He claims he can use them. He's the one who hired me."

"I was hired by a fella named Cory, Ed Cory. Claims him and your Weston are the organizers of this thing."

"They've got money men behind them, though."

"That's what I figured. Take a stroll around the grounds with me? I wanna see what I'm up against."

"Let's do it," Clint said.

FOUR

In circling the Fairground's they ran into Heck's three other security men. He introduced them to Clint, who shook hands with each of them.

"Wow," one of them said. "The Gunsmith. I heard you were gonna be a judge, but I didn't think it was true."

"Did you hear about any other judges?" Clint asked him.

"No," the young man said, "just you."

"Stay alert," Heck told them. "With this many guns around there's bound to be trouble."

All three men nodded. Clint filed away their first names for later—Tim, Frank, and Jimmy.

The first person Clint recognized, other than Heck, was Cole Weston.

"That's Weston," he told Heck as they approached the man.

"Look at them guns," Heck said. "He better be good with 'em."

"He probably is," Clint said, "target shooting. Don't know that he's ever had to fire at another man, though."

When Weston saw Clint he smiled.

"I'm so glad to see you," he said, rushing up to shake hands. "Welcome."

"You sound like you were afraid I wouldn't make it."

"Well . . . you always could have changed your mind," Weston said, "and I did sort of, uh, guarantee that you'd be here."

"Well, here I am," Clint said. "You know Heck Thomas, of course."

"Yes," Weston said, shaking hands with Heck. "I'm glad you're both here."

"Things look like they're coming along," Clint said.

The tables set up for registration seemed besieged by competitors.

"Yes, everyone's showin' up early to sign up," Weston said. "Our first contest doesn't go off until tomorrow at three."

"What about the other judges?"

"They're here," Weston said, excitedly.

"How many?"

"Two others," the man said. "We felt we only needed three judges."

"And who are the other two?"

"If you'll allow me," Weston said. "I'd like to hold that back until we all have supper together later."

"Me, I don't like surprises," Heck said. "I'll leave you two to your plans. I have some of my own. See you later, Clint. What hotel are you staying in?"

"The King Louis," Clint said.

"I'm down the street at the Napoleon," Heck said.

"Two good hotels," Weston said.

Heck went off to take care of his own business and Weston said to Clint, "I want you to meet my partner."

Weston led Clint over to the registration tables, where competitors were receiving numbers they would wear. Another man was standing nearby, wearing a single Colt on his left hip with a trick holster designed for a quick draw.

"Clint Adams, meet Ed Cory."

Cory, a few years older than Weston, extended his right hand, keeping his left free for his gun.

"Glad to meet you, Clint," he said.

"Interesting rig you have there," Clint said, eyeing the holster.

Rather than a full leather holster there were just a couple of loops holding the gun in place. Once the barrel cleared the bottom loop the gun could be positioned for use. Not having to draw the gun completely out of a leather holster saved a split second that would make the difference.

"Thanks. We have a fast-draw contest, and all's fair," Cory said. "We've got our share of spring-loaded holsters, but I thought I'd try this."

"So you're competing as well as organizing?" Clint asked.

"We both are," Weston said.

"And will all three judges be scoring all the events, or will we have events assigned to us?" Clint asked.

"We can talk that over at supper," Weston said. "Ed, Clint's at the King Louis, so I thought we'd eat at the Cajun Queen, down the street from there."

"Fine with me," Cory said. "At six?"

"That's good," Weston said. "Meet you there."

Supper was still a few hours away so Clint said, "That seems to leave me with some time to kill. Mind if I go to the races?"

"Go ahead," Weston said. "We still have some things to firm up here. Do you want to meet back here about five? Or just meet at the restaurant?"

"Let's meet at the restaurant," Clint suggested. "That way I can go back to my hotel and put on something a little more . . . appropriate."

"Yeah," Weston said, "we'll need to clean up a bit, as well."

"Okay, then," Clint said, "I'll pick a few winners and see you fellas later."

As he walked away, Ed Cory said to his partner, "You think he'll do it?"

"I hope so," Weston said. "This whole thing depends on it."

Cory nodded and said, "Let's finish signin' these people up."

FIVE

Clint returned to his hotel and washed some of the Fairgrounds off him. He had hit two winners that afternoon but ended up with plenty of both the field and the track on him and his clothes.

When he was dressed to go to supper he still had about twenty minutes before he had to walk to the restaurant. He opened the French doors and stepped out onto the gallery. He looked down at busy Bourbon Street, breathed in the mixed scents that made up the French Quarter—Cajun food, night-blooming jasmine and sweet olive blossoms, damp, money, cheap perfume, and . . . not-so-cheap perfume? Where was that coming from?

The gallery was common to all the rooms so he walked along until he came to the corner of Bourbon Street and Toulouse Street. The French doors to the corner room were open and the smell of expensive perfume was coming from within.

It wasn't quite dark out, and there were no lamps lit inside so he couldn't see into the darkened room. He turned his back to it and stared down at the street again.

He could also hear the sounds of several different kinds of music floating out over the streets.

"I love the Quarter," a woman's voice said from the darkness of the room.

"Excuse me?" He turned to peer into the room again.

"Oh, I'm sorry," she said. "I can see you out there but you can't see me in here, can you?"

He narrowed his eyes. He could make out an indistinct form, but that was all.

"No," he replied, "I can't see you but I can smell you."

"What do you smell?"

"I don't know the name of it," he confessed, "but I know it's expensive."

She laughed.

"How do you know that?"

"Because most of the perfume I smell in the Quarter is cheap."

"Maybe that's because of the quality of the women you keep the company of."

"Well, then," he said, "meeting you will be a big improvement, won't it?"

She laughed again.

"I suppose I should make it easy on you, then."

He watched as the woman appeared from the darkened room, stepping out onto the gallery.

"Well, good evening," Clint said.

"Good evening, sir."

"My name is Clint Adams."

"Mr. Adams," she said, "I am Kit Devereaux. Actually, it's Katherine."

"French?"

"Creole."

"From here?"

"Originally," she said, but offered no more.

She stepped to the railing, stood next to him. They both stared down at Bourbon Street.

"I still love the Quarter," she said.

"Still?"

"I used to love all New Orleans, and Louisiana, but now I am limited to the Quarter."

He turned his head to study her, and take in more of her scent.

She was tall, raven haired, with luminous pale skin and ruby red lips. She was wearing an off-the-shoulder blue gown that showed a tantalizing amount of her long, graceful neck, shoulders, and bosom.

"So you're here visiting family?"

"Not exactly," she said. "What brings you to the *Vieux Carré*?"

"I'm here for a shooting competition."

"The Louisiana Shoot-out I've heard about?"

"Heard where?"

"Everywhere. I've been here for two days and I've heard about it everywhere. Are you competing?"

"No," he said, "I'm one of the judges."

"Oh, I thought . . ."

"Thought what?"

"Well, I know who you are . . . I thought, with your reputation . . . But I guess it makes sense that you would be a judge. I mean, who could beat the Gunsmith?"

"I can think of a few people," he said, "but as a rule I don't compete with my gun."

"I guess you wouldn't have to."

He turned to face her.

"I have an appointment for supper with some people from the competition. Would you like to join us?"

"I have an appointment of my own tonight," she said, "but I wouldn't mind having supper with you another night."

"How about a drink later tonight?" he asked.

"That sounds even better. How about down the street at a place called Baptiste's?"

"At nine?"

"Nine is good," she said with a smile.

SIX

The Cajun Queen was a café/saloon with live music going at almost all times. As Clint entered, he noticed there were no girls working the floor, and no gambling. It was strictly a place people went to eat, drink, and listen to music.

He spotted Ed Cory and Cole Weston sitting at a table they had secured near the back of the room. As he reached them, Weston said, "We saved you the seat with your back to the wall."

"That was considerate," Clint said, taking the seat. "Thanks."

A waiter came over and Clint ordered a cold beer.

"We took the liberty of ordering po'boys and dirty rice," Weston said. "It's a local—"

"I know what a po'boy sandwich is, Cole," Clint said. "That's fine."

"Good."

"What did you think of our setup this afternoon?" Cory asked.

"The setup?" Clint asked after downing a swallow of beer. "All I saw was chaos."

Cory looked as if he'd been slapped.

"Well, yes, maybe it looked that way—"

Weston interrupted him with a laugh.

"Face it, Ed," he said. "It was chaotic. Pandemonium might even be a better word, but it will improve tomorrow."

"I'm sure it will," Clint said. "I didn't mean to insult anyone. I'm sorry."

"That's okay," Weston said. "Ed just gets a little . . . sensitive sometimes."

Cory was frowning, but he didn't argue.

"The competition begins tomorrow," Weston said. "The other judges have arrived. In the morning we'll let you know which contests you'll be judging, but we thought with you being who you are, we'd let you pick and choose."

"That's nice of you," Clint said, "but I don't want any special treatment. I'll take whichever contests you see fit."

"That's very cooperative of you, Mr. Adams," Cory said.

"You can call me Clint."

"Clint . . . I only wish the other judges were as easy to get along with as you are."

"Are they being difficult?"

"They are."

"That's not very nice of them," Clint said, "considering you're covering their expenses. Who are the other judges? Or is that still a secret?"

"It's not a secret," Weston said. "We just thought you should all meet, but . . ."

"But what?" Clint asked. "Wait, don't tell me. You invited them to eat with us, but they declined."

Cory and Weston exchanged a glance, and Weston said, "Yes, that's right."

"Do the other two judges know each other?"

"No."

"Have they seen each other?"

"No."

"And do they know about me yet?"

"No."

"Okay—" Clint started, but stopped when the waiter appeared with their food.

"Can we get three more beers?" Weston asked.

"Of course, sir."

"You were sayin'?" Weston asked.

"I was about to ask," Clint said, "the names of the other two judges."

"One of the judges is a man named Jack Vermillion," Weston said.

"Texas Jack?" Clint asked. "Ol' Shoot-Your-Eye-Out Vermillion?"

"You know him, then?"

"Yes," Clint said, "Jack and I know each other. Well enough, in fact, that I'm wondering why he'd agree to do this."

"Maybe you can ask him when you see him tomorrow," Cory said. "So far, he's been . . . disagreeable, and hasn't been talkin' to many people."

"The Jack I know can be . . . disagreeable at times," Clint said. "Who's the other judge?"

"We thought it would be a good idea to have a woman as a judge," Weston said, around a bite of po'boy.

"We have quite a few women who have signed up to compete," Cory said.

"Well, that should be interesting," Clint said. "Don't tell me you got Annie Oakley to come and be a judge?"

"No," Weston said, "although we did send a telegram invitin' her."

"Then who did you get?"

"Somebody who has quite a reputation locally," Weston said. "You probably never heard of her. Her name's Kit Devereaux."

SEVEN

When Clint walked into Baptiste's he saw a small, dark, comfortable, and quiet saloon. The bar was dark cherry wood and the bartender was dark as ebony. His sleeves were rolled up to reveal muscular forearms and biceps.

"Welcome to Baptiste's," the man said as Clint approached the bar. "I'm Baptiste, me."

The man had a true Cajun accent.

"My name is Clint Adams," Clint said. "I'm supposed to be meeting Katherine Devereaux for a drink."

"Ah, Kit," the man said, his eyes lighting up. Clint judged the man's age as between fifty and sixty. He had some white in his kinky black hair. "You're a lucky man, you. Our Kit doesn't drink with many men."

"Then I am lucky," Clint said. "I think I'll have a beer while I'm waiting for her."

"Comin' up."

Baptiste returned with a foaming, cold mug of beer and set it down in front of Clint.

"Best beer in Louisiana," he announced.

Clint tasted it, and nodded. He had to agree. The beer was wonderful.

"How long have you known Kit, you?" Baptiste asked him.

"Just met her tonight."

Baptiste looked impressed.

"And she has already agreed to drink wit' you?" he asked.

"Like you said," Clint replied. "I'm lucky."

"Your name sounds familiar to me," Baptiste admitted.

Clint looked around. There were several men in the place, all drinking and minding their own business.

"You might have hard of me," Clint said. "I'm here to judge the sharpshooting contest."

"Ah, that's why Kit is back in town, also," Baptiste said. Then he snapped his fingers and pointed a thick forefinger at Clint. "The Gunsmith, right? You're the Gunsmith, you."

"I am."

Baptiste started to laugh.

"What's so funny?"

"You better watch out for that gal," he said. "She'll want to shoot with you."

"We're both judges."

"I know," he said, "but she won't be able to resist the challenge."

"You think so?"

"I know so," he said. "I know Kit very well."

"How well?"

"Better than anyone," he said. "She's my daughter."

"Your daughter?"

"I know," he said, stroking his arm. "I'm black as coal and she's light skinned. Takes after her mother. Now she was a true beauty."

"Was?"

"She passed on more than ten years ago," Baptiste said.

"Was she sick?"

Baptiste seemed to tremble and he said, "I don't talk about that, me."

"I'm sorry," Clint said. "I didn't mean to pry."

The moment became awkward between them and they were saved by Kit's arrival.

"Well, I see you and Baptiste have met," she said, sidling up next to Clint.

She was wearing a different gown, this one green, but showing just as much skin.

"We've been having a nice talk," Clint said.

"Papa?" she asked. "What have you been saying to Clint?"

"Nothing but good things, me," Baptiste said, raising his eyebrows in an attempt to look innocent.

"Well, give the man another beer and I'll have a Napoleon brandy."

"You go and sit, you, and I will bring it to the table," the big black man said.

"Come along, Clint," she said, sliding her arm into his. He reached for his half-finished beer but she said, "Leave it. Papa will bring you a fresh one."

She led him to a table for two in a dark corner.

"You're a sneaky young lady," Clint said.

"Sneaky? How?"

"You didn't tell me you were a judge at the contest, even after I told you I was."

She looked amused.

"You didn't ask me," she said. "Did Papa tell you?"

"No," he said, "I heard from Weston and Cory."

"Ah . . ."

"They told me they invited you to supper and you turned them down."

"I don't like them," she said. "In fact, I don't like most men."

"And why is that?"

They were interrupted when Baptiste came over with their drinks.

"Thank you, Papa," Kit said.

Her father looked like he had something to say, but Clint thought the man looked as if he were afraid of his daughter, who was half his size.

He withdrew.

"He's the reason," she said.

"The reason for what?"

She sat back and sipped her brandy before answering the question.

"He's the reason I don't like most men."

"And why's that?"

"He killed my mother."

"What?"

"Oh," she said, "he didn't shoot her, or stab her, or strangle her, but he killed her."

"I don't understand," Clint said. "He said your mother

died, but when I asked if she's been sick he seemed to get upset."

"Yes," she said, "he gets very upset about it." She leaned forward and asked, "Wouldn't you be upset if you knew you killed your wife?"

EIGHT

"I'm sorry," Kit said. "I don't mean to bore you with my family history."

"I can listen," Clint said, "if you want to talk."

She eyed him across the table, then said, "I don't know why, but suddenly I do."

Clint sipped his beer and waited.

"My father believes in voodoo," she said. "He worships Marie Laveau. Do you know Marie Laveau?"

"I know of her," he said. "A voodoo priestess from years ago."

"Many people here and in the bayou believe she may still be alive."

"And your father is one of them?"

"Yes."

"But not your mother?"

Kit hesitated, then said, "On the contrary, my mother was a voodoo priestess herself."

"So they both believed in it."

"They both lived it."

"And you?"

"I was raised to believe in it," she said, "but when my mother died I stopped."

"So . . . how did your father contribute to your mother's death?"

When he asked the question, her eyes moved to the bar, where her father was serving drinks.

"I think I'll have to know you a little longer, a little better, before I tell you that, Mr. Adams."

"Then maybe you should start calling me Clint," he said.

"All right, Clint."

"Katherine," he said. "That's a beautiful name. Why Kit?"

"My father started calling me that when I was little," she said. "I liked it. I still do."

"So . . . when did you become interested in guns?"

Her face lit up.

"I'm fascinated by guns," she said. "The first time I ever held one I knew."

"Are we talking about handguns, rifles, what?"

"Pistols," she said. "I love the way they feel."

"How good are you with them?"

"Very good."

"How come I never heard of you?"

"I'm only known locally," she said. "Away from here I'm just a girl with an odd love of guns. Plus, I've never killed anyone. That's how you become known, isn't it?"

"I suppose it is."

Suddenly, she seemed afraid she had offended him.

"I'm sorry," she said, "I didn't mean—"

"Forget it," he said. "It is what I'm known for. There's no way around that. I've killed a lot of people, but never anyone who was innocent, or who wasn't trying to kill me."

She reached out and touched his hand.

"I believe you."

"So why did Weston and Cory ask you to be a judge?" he asked.

"Because I'm local, I guess," she said, "and because there will be women competing. They probably think it's only fair. I heard they tried to get Annie Oakley. I don't mind being second choice to her."

"She's a very good shot," he said. "Maybe the best I've ever seen."

"You know her?" she asked excitedly.

"I do," he said. "We're friends."

"And she's the best you've seen?" she asked. "Better than Wild Bill? Wyatt Earp? You?"

"Better shooting at targets," he qualified, "not at shooting men who are shooting back."

She nodded and sipped her drink.

NINE

Clint and Kit finished their drinks and went to the bar so she could say good night to her father. For someone who blamed her mother's death on her father, she seemed to get along with him pretty well.

"Good night, Papa."

"Good night, Baptiste," Clint said. "It was nice to meet you."

"And you, too, Mr. Gunsmith," Baptiste said.

They left Baptiste's and walked to the hotel with Kit's arm linked in Clint's left arm.

"Do you have a gun on you?" he asked.

"Where would I keep a gun?"

"I was just wondering," he said.

They walked a block before she said, "Actually, I do. I have a two-shot derringer on my left thigh."

"I thought so."

"How did you know?"

"It's the way you're walking."

"You have good eyes."

When they reached the hotel, they went up to the second floor together and he walked her to her door.

"I talked to you more tonight than I've talked to any man," she said.

"I was interested," he said. "I hope it did you some good."

"Maybe," she said, "it made me realize that there are some good men left."

She kissed him on the cheek and went into her room. He stood there for a moment, then turned and walked down the hall to his own room.

Clint hung his gun belt on the bedpost, removed his boots and pants. He was about to get into bed when there was a knock on the French doors from the gallery. He pulled his gun from his holster, walked to the doors, and looked out.

He opened the door and Kit stood there, naked.

"You're crazy," he said. "Anybody could've seen you out there."

She laughed and said, "I want you to see me."

"Oh, I see you."

"Are you going to shoot me," she asked, "or let me in?"

Kit helped Clint out of the remainder of his clothes. They left the French doors open. It let in a breeze, and the moonlight. By the silver light he admired her high, small but firm breasts, slender waist, and long, lovely legs. When she turned his eyes followed the beautiful line of her back down to her taut butt.

When she slid off his underwear, his erection popped

up, demanding her attention, and she gave it. She clasped it in both hands, first stroking it, then lending her mouth to the action. She licked the head, up and down the shaft, pressed it to her lips, then opened her mouth and took him in.

He groaned as she accommodated his entire length, sucking him wetly. She clasped his ass with both hands as her head bobbed up and down on him. She moaned, slid her hands up and down the backs of his thighs, dug her nails in there. Then she brought one hand around to cup his testicles as she continued to suck him.

Abruptly, he reached down to her, slid his hands beneath her arms and pulled her to her feet. He kissed her, thrusting his tongue into her mouth. She moaned and opened herself to him. He slid his hand between them and slipped his fingers between her legs. He found her wet and waiting. Gently, he slid a finger along her moist slit, then inside her. She gasped into his mouth. He broke the kiss, lifted her into his arms and carried her to the bed.

He set her down gently, stood up straight, and stared down at her. She gazed back up at him, her arms extended over her head, one leg bent at the knee. The moonlight was making her pale skin almost translucent, and her brown nipples even darker.

He got on the bed with her and began moving his mouth over her incredibly smooth skin. She moaned as he kissed her breasts and her neck, her shoulders, her mouth, back to her breasts again where he licked and nibbled her nipples. She cradled his head while he worked on her breasts for a little while, and then he ventured lower. Finally, he was on his knees between her legs.

"Oh," she said as he leaned in and licked her, "oh, my, yes . . ." She went on. "Ooh!"

He got down on his belly and chest, slid his hands beneath her buttocks, lifted her up off the bed, and set about thoroughly enjoying himself.

TEN

In a saloon on N. Rampart and Esplanade, the very north-eastern tip of the French Quarter, Ed Cory was meeting with two men. His partner in the Louisiana Shoot-out had no idea who these men were, or that they were the main investors in the contest.

"What took you so long?" Victor Newman asked. At fifty, he was one of the wealthiest men in Louisiana, but for some reason his wealth was not making him happy.

"I had supper with my partner and Clint Adams," Cory said, seating himself. "After Adams left Cole still wanted to talk. He's . . . enthusiastic."

"He's a fool," the other man said. He was forty-eight, not as wealthy as Victor Newman, but just as unhappy. He was, however, from one of the wealthier families in New Orleans—the DuBois family.

"The idiot could end up getting in our way," Anton DuBois said.

"I can handle Cole," Cory assured them.

"Can you handle Clint Adams?"

"Yes."

"And the other man?" Newman asked.

"Texas Jack?" Cory said. "Of course. I can not only handle him, but I can pretty much control him."

"And the woman?" DuBois asked.

"Well," Cory said, "what woman is controllable?"

"Why did you invite her, anyway?" DuBois asked.

"That was Weston's idea, and he did it without consulting me."

"Never mind," Newman said. "She won't be a problem. We can see to that."

"How?" Cory asked.

Newman smiled.

"We have our own people who are good with a gun."

"Don't forget," DuBois said, "the field will be full of people—men and women—who can use a gun."

"To shoot at targets," Newman said. "Very few of them have ever had to shoot at another person, let alone someone shooting at them."

"And your people?" Cory asked.

"My people have killed many times," Newman said, "and they are the most reliable of all killers—the kind who do it for money."

"All right, then," DuBois said. "The contests begin tomorrow. When does our plan go into effect?"

Newman looked at Cory.

"That will be up to our friend, here," he said. "We're going to send a little insurance with you."

"Insurance?" Ed Cory asked. "How do you mean?"

Newman waved. A man disengaged himself from the bar he'd been leaning on and walked over. He was tall, in his late thirties, had a Colt on his right hip in a worn leather holster. He looked critically at the ornate design on the butt of Cory's gun.

"Pretty," he said.

"Ed Cory, meet Dave Kendrick," Newman said. "He will be your right-hand man from now on—at least, from now until our partnership ends."

"I don't need a bodyguard," Cory said.

"Really?" Kendrick asked with a laugh. "You sure look like you could use one."

Cory looked up at the man and said, "I can handle myself."

"You may be a marksman, Cory," Newman said, "but Kendrick is a gunman. There's a big difference."

"See?" Kendrick said, indicating his holster. "No pretty gun here, just one that kills."

"Okay," Cory said, "this is not going to look good, having a killer follow me around."

"Well then," Newman said, "enter him in the contest. You can do that, can't you?"

"Well sure, but . . ."

"I don't wanna be in no damn contest with a bunch of amateurs," Kendrick said.

"Why not?" Victor Newman asked. "Afraid they'll show you up?"

"Hell, no—"

"You don't have to win anything," Newman went on, "just . . . be around."

"You can do that, can't you?" Cory asked Kendrick.

"I can shoot with anybody," Kendrick said, "don't you worry about that."

"Good," Newman said, "then that settles it. Kendrick, be on the grounds tomorrow morning."

"Better come at nine a.m.," Cory said reluctantly. "I'll get you signed up."

He rose, standing an inch or two shorter than the gunman.

"You gents have nothin' to worry about," he said. "Everythin' is gonna work out fine."

He turned and left the saloon.

"Is he going to last?" DuBois asked.

"I think we'll just have to wait and see," Newman said.

"You mind if I have a drink with you?" Kendrick asked.

"Yes," Newman said, "I do mind. I don't drink with the help. Go back to the bar, Kendrick. I'll call you when I need you."

Kendrick hesitated, but in the end it was his greed that won out. He didn't want to do anything that would stop Newman from paying him.

"Sure," Kendrick said, "sure."

He turned and walked back to the bar.

"You want to push him that far?" DuBois asked. "He looks mean."

"I pay him to look mean," Newman said. "And as long as I pay him, he'll continue to look mean somewhere else."

"I hope you're right."

"Of course I'm right, Anton," Newman said. "It's all about money. It's always all about money."

"I'll try to remember that."

"You do that."

ELEVEN

A high, keening sound came from Kit's mouth. She grabbed Clint's head with both hands and closed her thighs on him. As his mouth worked on her avidly, eagerly lapping up her delicious juices, she bit her lips to keep herself from screaming.

"Ooh, God," she said, "I'm burning up. You're making me . . . I'm going to lose my . . . mind."

But it wasn't her mind she lost. It was control of her body, which began to buck and jerk beneath him. He pinned down her thighs using his elbows, continued to lick and suck as waves of pleasure washed over her.

He felt her belly trembling and, if possible, she was going to lose control even more. He quickly removed his face from her crotch, straddled her, gripped her by the ankles, spread her, and drove his rigid cock into her.

Her eyes popped wide open, as did her mouth, but no sound came out. He began to thrust himself in and out of her powerfully. Her cries were loud, but there was still music and laughter coming from the street, so even with the French doors open people wouldn't hear her. Or if they did, they wouldn't care.

Pretty soon he was grunting with the effort of chasing his own relief, so now both of them were making noise. It was possible someone in the rooms on either side of Clint's could hear them, but then they'd probably think the noise was coming from the street.

Of course, if anyone stepped out onto the gallery . . .

Later they were lying in his bed together, her head on his shoulder.

"I have to go back to my room," she said suddenly, sitting up.

The sweat on their bodies had not quite dissipated, and they could both feel the breeze from outside cooling them.

"Why?" he asked.

"We both have to get up early for the shoot-out," she said.

"So? Spend the night here."

"I can't," she said. "I . . . it's something about me . . . I just . . . I can't sleep in a bed with anyone else with me."

"Okay."

"I had to share a bed through most of my childhood," she went on. "I just . . . I just can't . . . do it anymore."

"There's no need to explain," he said. "Go on. I'll see you in the morning."

She leaned over and kissed him.

"Thank you."

As she headed for the door, he yelled, "Hey!"

She turned.

He tossed her his shirt.

"Wear that back to your room," he said. "You can give it back to me in the morning."

She caught the shirt and smiled.

"Such a gentleman."

She pulled the shirt on, held it closed, and stepped out onto the gallery.

Clint got out of bed, walked to the doors, and pulled them closed. He locked them securely, then returned to the bed.

He rolled himself up in the sheets that held her fragrance, and fell asleep.

TWELVE

The next morning Clint rose early enough to have breakfast before heading out to the Fairgrounds for the first day of the competition. He thought about knocking on Kit's door—the French doors, as she had done the night before—but decided against it. Kit seemed to have some issues she needed to deal with. He decided that letting her call the tune while he danced the dance was worth it—for now.

When he reached the Fairgrounds—or the grounds adjacent to the Fairgrounds racetrack—he saw that competitors were still signing up. Others were milling about, checking their rifles and handguns to make sure they were working properly. Clint saw enough pearl handles and ornate filigree to blind him. He never put much stock in anybody who had to decorate their firearms.

He saw Cole Weston standing off to one side talking to a tall, rangy man he recognized as Texas Jack Vermillion. He walked over to join them.

"Texas Jack," Clint said, slapping the man on the back.

Vermillion turned quickly, his hand streaking toward his gun, and stopped short when he saw Clint.

"Adams," he said. "They told me you were one of the judges. I didn't believe 'em."

"Yeah, well, same here, Jack," Clint said. "I can't figure out why you'd do something like this."

"Ah, why not?" Vermillion said. "I got nothin' else to do, and I like this town."

"I've gotta go and find our third judge," Weston said. "Will you gents excuse me?"

"Sure, go ahead," Vermillion said. "Clint and me gotta catch up."

As Weston left, Vermillion asked Clint, "You know who the third judge is?"

"A gal named Katherine Devereaux."

"I heard it was a Kit Devereaux."

"Same girl."

"I never heard of her."

"She's local."

"Is she any good with a gun?"

"So I've heard, but I haven't seen her shoot."

"You know they got women in this contest?" Vermillion asked.

"I heard that," Clint said. "I suppose that's why they wanted one of the judges to be a woman."

"A woman can't outshoot a man," Vermillion said.

"I guess we'll have to wait and see," Clint said. He didn't bother mentioning Annie Oakley to Texas Jack.

"Look at all these amateurs," Vermillion said, looking around. "All those pearl handles are blindin' me."

"I know what you mean," Clint said.

"They ain't impressin' me with fancy guns," Vermillion said. "They damn well better know how to shoot."

"That's what it's all about, Jack," Clint said. "The shooting."

Clint spotted Weston returning, with Kit Devereaux behind him. She was covered up today, wearing jeans and a man's shirt, and even a hat. She also had a gun strapped to her hip.

"Here comes our other judge."

Vermillion turned to look, and caught his breath.

"Jesus . . ." he said.

"I know."

"Still," Vermillion said, "a woman that looks like that probably can't shoot."

"Gentlemen," Cole Weston said, "meet our third judge, Miss Kit Devereaux. Kit, meet Jack Vermillion."

"Texas Jack," Vermillion said, taking her hand. "A pleasure."

Clint was surprised at Jack's sudden transformation into a gentleman.

"And Clint Adams."

"Oh," Kit said, "Clint and I have already met."

"You have?" Weston asked.

"We're staying in the same hotel," Clint said.

At that point Ed Cory came over.

"Good, you're all together," he said. "Did you tell them?"

"I was about to," Weston said.

"Tell us what?" Vermillion asked.

"We've decided to conduct our contests one at a time, so that all three judges can vote."

"Are we still starting today at three?" Kit asked.

"Today," Cory said, "at one."

"That still gives us a couple of hours to finish signin' people up," Weston said.

"Which is what we're gonna go and do right now," Cory said.

"We'd appreciate it if the three of you would not stray too far away," Weston said.

The three judges exchanged a glance, and then Clint said, "We'll be around."

THIRTEEN

The three judges stood off to one side and watched some of the contestants practicing, shooting at targets.

"They're terrible," Vermillion said.

"That's probably why they're practicing," Kit observed.

Vermillion looked at her and said, "You know, you and me might get along."

"According to our esteemed hosts," Clint said to Vermillion, "you're being disagreeable, Jack."

"Disagreeable?"

"You refused to have supper with them—with us—last night?"

"Hey, I agreed to be a judge," Vermillion said. "That don't mean I have to eat with those two dudes."

"He has a point," Kit said. "I don't really want to eat with them, either—especially not the one with the pearl handles."

"See?" Vermillion said. "There's a woman after my own heart."

"Don't count on it," Kit said to him, but she was grinning.

Vermillion pointed to the gun on her hip. It had a plain wooden handle, was not fancy but was well kept.

"Can you use that?" he asked.

"I can hit what I shoot at," she said.

"Targets?" Vermillion asked.

"That is what we're talking about, isn't it?" she asked. "Targets?"

"That's what this is all about," Clint said.

"I was never real good at target shootin' myself," Vermillion said. "I tend to shoot better when I'm bein' shot at."

"Well," Kit said, also being honest, "I've never been shot at, so I don't know how I would perform in that situation."

"I've seen Clint shoot the middle out of a two-bit piece that's been tossed into the air," Vermillion said. "Can you do that?"

"Hmm," she said. "I've done it with a dollar piece, but I've never tried with two bits."

"Why don't we try it right now?" Vermillion asked.

"But we're not competing," she pointed out.

"I know," Vermillion said, "but I'm just kind of . . . curious."

Kit looked at Clint.

"You don't have to if you don't want to," he said.

"Looks like there's room over there," she said, pointing at an area of the field that wasn't in use. "I'm willing if you are."

"No, not Clint," Vermillion said, "you. I know what

he can do." He put his hand in his pocket and came out with a coin. "I got two bits."

"Okay, then," Kit Devereaux said. "Let's go."

They walked over to the empty section of the field, but their movements did not go unnoticed. Some of the contestants seemed to realize something was going on and they drifted over to watch.

"Okay," Vermillion said, moving away from Kit, "get yerself set."

"Do you want me to draw and fire?" she asked. "Or just fire?"

"Make it easy on yerself."

She took her gun out, held it down at her side, and waited.

Vermillion held the two-bit piece in his hand.

"Ready?"

"When you are."

"Toss it nice and high, Jack," Clint said. He knew it would make an easier target if she could see the sun glinting off it.

"Call it, Clint," Vermillion said.

"On three," Clint said. "One . . . two . . . three!"

Vermillion tossed the coin high into the air. The sun glinted off it, several of the bystanders pointed up at it, others yelled.

Kit tried to block them all out. She followed the flight of the coin, brought her pistol up, and tried to fire just as the coin reached its zenith, just when it might have been floating there, motionless, not rising, not falling, just for a split second.

The report of her pistol came first and then the coin

seemed to jerk in the air. When it fell to the ground, Vermillion went over and picked it up.

"She hit it," he yelled, holding it up, "but not dead center."

He carried it over to her, and Clint joined him. There was a smattering of applause. Vermillion handed Kit the coin, and she held it in her palm. The bullet had taken a piece off the coin, but that was it.

"That's a hit," Vermillion said.

"But like you said," she pointed out, "not dead center."

"In other words," Clint said, "not a winning shot, if you were competing."

Kit looked at Vermillion and asked, "You got another coin?"

FOURTEEN

Jack Vermillion took his place again and waited for Clint to count it off.

"One . . . two . . . three!"

Vermillion tossed the coin, it glinted. Kit fired and the coin fell to the ground.

"A clean miss," Vermillion said when he picked it up. "First time must have been a fluke."

"Toss it again!" Kit yelled.

Clint looked around. The crowd was larger after the miss than it had been after she'd clipped the first coin.

"Kit, why don't we—"

"Toss it!" she said to Vermillion.

"Okay."

He tossed the coin again. Kit fired, and missed.

"It's too small," she said. "Toss a silver dollar."

"Honey," Jack Vermillion said, "I ain't got a silver dollar."

"Well, that's too small."

Vermillion walked over to her and said, "Hey, you hit it once out of three."

"That's not the way to win a contest," someone shouted.

Kit looked out at the crowd and said, "You try it."

Nobody stepped up. Apparently they didn't want to give away what they could or could not do before the contest started.

"I'll bet Clint can do it."

Clint looked over to see who had spoken. It was Ed Cory.

"Whataya say, Clint?" Cory asked. "Show these people how it's done?"

"It can't be done!" someone yelled. "It's too damn small."

"Come on, Clint," Cory said. "It'll inspire all these people to compete."

Clint looked at Vermillion, who was tossing the coin up and catching it. He raised his eyebrows and Clint just nodded.

Vermillion walked out into the middle of the field.

"Who's gonna count it off?" he asked.

"Forget it," Clint said, "just toss it."

Vermillion did, as high as he could.

Clint drew and fired. The coin jumped even higher as his bullet struck it. As the coin started to fall, he fired again and the coin jumped again. He was going to fire a third time but stopped himself.

The coin fell to the ground. Vermillion walked over and picked it up. He stood there, staring at it, then carried it to Clint.

"One hole," he said.

"Ha!" someone shouted. "A hit and a miss!"

Clint took the coin, looked at it, then handed it back to Vermillion.

"Not bad," Jack said. "One direct hit, one miss."

Kit came over and took the coin.

"Look at it closely," Clint said.

Ed Cory walked over as well, followed by Cole Weston.

"This hole is not round," Kit said, "it's oblong. See?" She handed the coin to Cory.

"I'll be damned," he said, holding it and up and peering through it. "He did it twice. Dead through the middle . . . twice! If he'd hit it once, the hole would be round."

"Give it to me," Weston said. "I want to pass it around."

He took the coin, handed it to someone, and then it started to circulate through the crowd.

"Two hits," someone said aloud, "and he fired from the hip."

The applause started slowly, then filtered through the crowd until they were all clapping their hands.

Clint ejected the spent shells, loaded live ones in, and holstered the gun. Seeing him do that, Kit did the same to her gun.

"One out of three really wasn't bad," he told her.

"Are you kidding?" she asked. "I did get lucky. But you? That was the most amazing display of marksmanship I've ever seen."

Clint looked at Cory.

"Hadn't you better get your people organized?" he asked.

"Yeah," Cory said. "I think you really inspired them, Clint."

Cory walked away and began herding the crowd.

Vermillion looked at Clint and said, "You might have inspired some of them, but I think you mighta scared the rest."

"Demoralized," Kit said.

"Yeah," Vermillion said, "that's what I meant."

"It was silly," Clint said. "I never should have done it."

"Well," Kit said, "you proved it could be done, and it wasn't a fluke."

"We better find out where we're supposed to be," Clint said and walked away.

FIFTEEN

"See that fella over there?" Vermillion said to Clint.

"Which one?"

"Black hat, black vest," Vermillion said. "Dressed like somebody told him that's the way a gunfighter dresses."

"Guess he went the other way," Clint said. "Instead of the pearl handles, he went for the clothes."

"Except for one thing."

"What's that?"

"He's a pro."

"What?"

"His name is Dave Kendrick," Vermillion said. "He hires his gun out."

"How much?"

"Whatever he can get," Vermillion said. "A nickel, if that's all that's available."

"So what's he doing competing in a competition like this?" Clint asked.

"That's a good question."

"What are you two talking about?" Kit asked, sitting down between them.

They were seated at the judges' table together, while the competitors for the first contest set up in front of them.

"Hello there, Kit," Clint said.

"What have we got here?" Kit asked.

"Playin' cards," Vermillion said. "They're gonna start with aces, move to deuces, keep goin' until somebody misses."

"What happens if they get to the paint cards?" she asked.

"Maybe we'll find out," Clint said.

They managed to rig a table to hold playing cards so they'd stand up face out. The table had enough cracks in it for the cards to be fitted into.

The competitors stood three abreast, with the aces—hearts, spades, diamonds—set up on the table.

"On the count of three you all fire," Cory said. "The first man who misses is eliminated. Ready?"

The three men nodded.

"On three. One . . . two . . . three!"

It was not a fast-draw competition, but one of the men chose to draw and fire, and he missed the spade in the center of his card.

The other two men were more deliberate. They aimed and fired, and each man pierced his card in the center.

"Next shooter," Cory called.

The man who missed stepped away and was replaced by a woman. The aces were replaced by deuces, so each shooter was going to have to fire twice.

It went on like that, with one shooter falling by the wayside each time. By the time the cards on the table reached sixes, each shooter had to empty their gun.

"Four hits on two cards, five on another," Cory said as he studied the cards. "All three shooters are eliminated."

"Hey," one of the shooters said, "I got five out of six. That ain't good enough?"

"No," Cory said. "It ain't."

Grumbling, the man left the line.

"We're putting seven up now," Cory shouted. "You must fire, reload, and fire from here on in. Speed is not a factor."

Three new shooters stepped up. One of them was Dave Kendrick. He very coolly fired six shots, reloaded, and fired a seventh. He hit the target seven times.

"There's something I don't understand," Kit said, leaning over toward Clint.

"What's that?"

"What is it we're judging?" she asked. "They either hit, or they don't."

"Good point. I guess we'll just have to wait for someone to ask us our opinion."

"Who came up with this idea?" she asked.

"One of our hosts, I guess."

She looked at the people who were waiting their turn to shoot.

"I don't think we're going to get to the picture cards."

It took a couple of hours to whittle the contest down to two men. One of them was Kendrick. The other was a man named Phil Locken. He was about five foot six and wore two guns. He was not allowed to use the second gun. He had to fire the first, reload, and fire again. He and Kendrick went through the nines and the tens.

Jacks next.

Cory came walking over to the judges' table.

"Any of you have any ideas?" he asked.

"About what?" Clint asked.

"We never figured to get this far," he said. "We thought we'd have a winner by the sixes and sevens. How do we do this with picture cards?"

Vermillion and Kit looked at Clint.

"What are you looking at me for?"

SIXTEEN

It took Clint a few minutes to come up with a solution.

"Put up more tens, and start again with the aces next to them. You don't need to use picture cards."

"If we get to threes again," Vermillion said, "tens and threes, they'll have to reload twice."

"Unless you let them use two guns," Kit added.

"That would give Locken an advantage over Kendrick," Clint said. "He wears two guns anyway, and Kendrick doesn't."

"Kendrick's a pro," Vermillion pointed out. "Why not give him the choice?"

"If he wants to win," Kit said, "he'll be against it. I would be."

Vermillion and Clint shared a look behind her back.

"Okay," Cory said. "I'll ask him."

He walked over to the two men, had a short conversation with them, and then came walking back.

"Kendrick said it's okay with him," Cory said. "We just need to loan him a second gun."

"He's okay with this?" Kit asked. "And he's willing to use a strange gun?"

Cory shrugged.

"He doesn't seem to care very much."

"Then why did he sign up?" Kit asked.

Vermillion and Clint exchanged another look.

Exactly.

They found Dave Kendrick a second gun, which he tucked into his gun belt. Phil Locken was looking very confident, checking both his guns while they were finding a second weapon for Kendrick.

Now they were standing together, eyeing their targets—ten and ace of hearts for Kendrick, ten and ace of spades for Locken.

"Ready?" Cory asked.

"What's Kendrick going to do?" Kit asked. "He's not used to firing with both hands."

Clint saw where Kendrick had put the second gun. It was sticking out of his belt, but it wasn't turned for a left-hand draw, it was turned for a right.

"I think I know."

The next few moments proved him correct.

"Go!" Cory shouted.

Locken was so confident that he drew with both hands and fired. Meanwhile, Kendrick drew his gun from his holster, fired all six shots, then returned it to his holster and drew the second gun. Locken finished shooting and turned his head to watch Kendrick fire his second gun.

"Hey . . ." he yelled.

Cory eyed the targets and said, "Twelve hits on the hearts, eleven hits on the spades. Kendrick wins."

"No, no, no," Locken complained. "He didn't draw and fire with both hands."

"That wasn't a rule," Clint said from the judges' table. "All he agreed to do was use a second gun. Nobody said he had to fire them at the same time."

"What the hell—"

"Clint's right," Kit said.

Cole Weston walked to the judges' table.

"Do you agree, Mr. Vermillion?" he asked.

"I agree," Vermillion said.

"The judges rule," Weston announced. "Kendrick wins. Let's move on to the next contest."

The three judges went to one of the wooden booths that had been erected to serve food and drinks. There was no beer, but someone had mixed together some icy punch, and all they really needed was something cold.

"That Locken was not a happy man," Kit said.

"But how about Kendrick?" Vermillion asked. "Guess he cared about winning, after all."

"He came up with a sound plan."

As they talked about him, Dave Kendrick came walking over to the booth and got some punch for himself. Then he turned to the three judges.

"Thanks for seein' my way," he said.

"It was a sound plan," Clint said.

He looked at the way Kit was eyeing Dave Kendrick. Apparently, she liked what she saw. Kendrick was tall, with thick shoulders, a lot of wavy black hair, and a mouth that had a cruel twist to the right.

"You were very impressive," she told him.

"That little peckerhead was impressive," he said. "He

sure could shoot with two hands. He was just a hair off on the ace."

"A hair's all it takes," Vermillion said.

"Well," Kendrick said, looking down at the second gun in his belt, "I got to give this back. Thanks again."

He turned and walked away.

"He's not like all these others," Kit observed.

"You're right about that," Clint said, but she didn't know how right she was.

SEVENTEEN

The second contest involved glass balls that would be tossed into the air. They were about the size of baseballs.

"Those will be a lot easier to hit than a two-bit piece," Kit observed.

"Kit," Clint said, "I didn't mean to try to show—"

She put her hand on his arm to stop him.

"Don't worry, Clint," she said. "I know what I'm capable of, and you know what you're capable of. What you did was . . . amazing."

"Hittin' that two-bit piece once was amazin', too," Vermillion pointed out.

"Thank you, Jack," she said.

This time the contest was being run by Weston. His partner, Cory, watched from the sidelines. They had two men standing by to throw the glass balls into the air.

"You'll shoot by twos," Weston explained. "First one to miss is out. Meanwhile, we'll keep count. The man—or woman—who shatters the most without a miss will win."

Kit sat back in her chair.

"I'm still wondering what we're doing here."

"Hey, we had to make a rulin' this morning with the cards," Vermillion said. "Judges rule, remember?"

"That's true."

Still, Clint was also wondering why Weston and Cory had decided they needed judges for these contests, when for the most part the winner would be clear. Like with these glass balls. Whoever shattered the most without a miss would win. Where was the need for a judge here?

The contest started, and the air was filling with the sound of shots and shattering glass. As a shooter missed, he was replaced. Eventually, Dave Kendrick toed the line and began shooting at glass balls. He was deadly accurate with a handgun; he had proven that twice now, with the cards and the balls. Clint wondered how he would be with a rifle. He hoped that the next contest on the agenda would be with rifles, just for a change.

The shattering of the balls went on all afternoon. Cory came over to the judges' table and said, "We have to start another contest. This one's goin' on too long."

"Some of these people are good shots," Vermillion said.

"Yeah, but the ones who're done can start on the next one. I figure we need two judges to come with me, and one of you can stay here."

"I'll stay," Vermillion said. "I wanna see who wins this thing."

"Okay, then," Cory said. "Clint, Kit, you can come with me. We got a rifle shoot to put on."

Clint stood up, pulled Kit's chair out as she stood. They followed Cory over to another section of the field where targets had been set up for shooters who were lined up. Just judging from the distance the shooters were from the targets, Clint would have known this part involved rifles. They were too far away for pistols.

There was another judges' table set up, so Clint and Kit sat down.

"This contest is two parts," he called out. "First stationary targets, then moving targets. You'll fire, reload, and fire at the stationary targets until you miss one. Then you'll step aside and let someone else shoot."

The targets were a collection of tin cans that had obviously been hoarded for a long time. Clint wondered why, if they had the money to buy the glass balls, they hadn't bought better targets for this.

The firing started and the field soon filled with the sounds of shots, lead hitting tin cans, and white smoke.

Miss . . . step aside . . .

Miss . . . step aside . . .

Miss . . . step aside . . .

"I didn't realize this could be so monotonous," Kit said to Clint, "and boring."

"Maybe tomorrow there will be something involving trick shooting," Clint said. "At least then we'd have something to watch."

"Trick shooting!" Kit exclaimed. "The balls and the cards? That wasn't trick shooting?"

"No, that's just considered marksmanship, Kit," Clint said.

"And the coin?"

"A little harder," he said, "but still marksmanship."

"Oh."

Clint looked back out at the contestants, but he was starting to wonder not only why they needed judges for this competition, but why they had chosen Kit Devereaux, who obviously was not the marksman—or markswoman—she was supposed to be.

EIGHTEEN

As contestants were eliminated from the glass ball contest, they moved over to the rifle shooting. Clint noticed both Dave Kendrick and the two-gun-wearing Phil Locken taking their places on the lines with rifles.

"Looks like they didn't fare so well with the glass balls," he said to Kit.

"Yeah, they did," Jack Vermillion said, taking the chair next to Kit. "We just finished over there and they finished first and second."

"Kendrick won that, too?" Kit asked.

"No," Vermillion said, "this time it was Locken who finished first."

"So those two are way ahead at this point."

"Looks like it," Vermillion said. "Let's see how they can do with rifles."

They watched as the two men fired, and before long they had both missed and were out.

"Not as good with rifles as they are with pistols," Kit said. "Excuse me."

They watched as she got up and hurried over to talk with Dave Kendrick.

"I hope you two weren't, um, involved," Vermillion said. "Miss Devereaux seems to have her eye on the professional killer."

"No," Clint said, "no involvement."

"What is it about killers that attracts women?" Vermillion asked.

"Some women find it exciting, I guess," Clint said. "Could be the killing, or the guns—"

"I wear a gun," Vermillion said. "Women don't seem to be throwing themselves at me."

Clint looked at Vermillion who, at best, was a homely man.

"You never know," he said.

"What?"

"We're in New Orleans," Clint said. "Anything can happen."

Kit put her arm through Kendrick's and the two of them walked off.

"She's supposed to be doin' her job," Vermillion said.

"It's getting later," Clint said. "I think our hosts might be ready to call it a day."

Cory and Weston were standing off to the side with their heads together.

"Looks like we're down to three shooters," Clint said. "My guess is we're almost done."

"Good," Vermillion said, "I'm starving."

"Eating alone again tonight?"

"You got another idea?"

"I might," Clint said, "I just might."

• • •

When the last shot was fired, Cory stepped forward and called a halt to the day.

"The moving target segment will begin at nine a.m.," he said. "If you miss the start, you'll be disqualified."

"What hotel are you staying at?" Clint asked Vermillion.

"They put me in a place on Royal."

"Let's ride back to the Quarter together," Clint said. "I know a good place to eat and drink."

"Sounds good," Vermillion said as they both stood up. "What about our, uh, fellow judge?"

"I think she has plans of her own for the night," Clint said.

NINETEEN

After a few mugs of beer, a steak dinner, and a few more mugs of beer, Jack Vermillion said, "This place is great! What's it called again?"

"Lafitte's Steak House," Clint said.

"What's a Lafitte?"

"He was a French pirate who was supposed to have been friends with Napoleon and Andrew Jackson."

"Andrew Jackson," Vermillion said. "I know who he is. Who was this Napoleon guy?"

"Never mind," Clint said. "Come on. We've got another place to hit."

"I like this place. Great beer."

"The next place has great beer," Clint said, "and great women."

"Now that sounds like a great idea!" Vermillion said. "Lead the way."

Outside on Royal Street, Clint told Vermillion they could walk to their next destination on Decatur. It was close enough, and he also thought the air would help Vermillion sober up a bit.

• • •

When they entered the house on Decatur, the madam came rushing up to them.

"Clint Adams, my *chéri*, it has been so long."

Clint hugged Madam Monique and couldn't quite get his arms all the way around her. "You have finally come to try one of my girls?"

"I told you, Monique," he said, "I'm waiting for you."

"Ah, my days of being in bed with a man are long over," she said. "Who is your friend?"

"This is Texas Jack Vermillion, madam," he said. "I was telling him about your beer, and your women."

She looked Vermillion up and down and asked, "And which one would you like to try first?"

"Uh, I think I'll start with a beer."

Madam Monique waved a bejeweled hand. "Go into the sitting room and I will have it brought to you. Meanwhile, you can become acquainted with my girls."

As she moved away, Vermillion grabbed Clint's arm and hissed, "You brought me to a whorehouse?"

"Come on, Jack," Clint said, "you've been in a whorehouse before, haven't you?"

"I'm a Methodist, Adams," Vermillion said. "I don't go to places like this."

Clint looked at Vermillion and asked, "Really?"

"Hell, yeah."

"You'll drink and curse, and you'll shoot somebody's eye out," Clint said, referring to an incident that earned Vermillion his nickname "Shoot-Your-Eye-Out," "but you won't go to a whorehouse?"

"What's your point?"

"Let's go inside and drink our beer," Clint said. "You

don't have to be with one of the girls if you don't want to."

"Have you ever been with one of these girls?" Vermillion asked.

"I don't usually pay for girls," Clint said, "but I doubt that any of these girls were here when I was here the last time."

They pushed aside a curtain and entered the sitting room, which was filled with men and scantily clad girls.

"Oh, Lord . . ." Vermillion said.

"Sorry, Jack," Clint said. "My mistake, I guess."

The beer was good, the women were better, but neither Clint nor Vermillion were tempted. Well, they were tempted, but they didn't give in.

However, they drank, danced with the girls to music played by an excellent piano player, and generally had a great time in a whorehouse without going upstairs with any of the girls.

When they left the house, the girls kissed both men on the cheek and begged them to come back the next night for "more fun."

"Those were nice girls," Vermillion said as they walked down Decatur Street.

"Maybe it's because they didn't have to go upstairs to work with us," Clint said. "They just had to stay downstairs and have some fun. It isn't often a man goes into a whorehouse and just dances with a girl."

"Those poor gals," Vermillion said. "They shouldn't have to have sex with a man unless they want to."

"That's a nice thought, Jack," Clint said. "If these girls

could go and get other jobs, I'm sure they would. Right now, though, their job is sex."

They stopped at Vermillion's hotel on Royal, said good night, and Clint continued on to his hotel on Bourbon Street.

TWENTY

When Clint got back to his room, he once again stepped outside onto the gallery to look down at Bourbon Street. Even last night, when he was in bed with Kit, he could hear activity on the street. Bourbon Street was a street that never slept.

He looked down the gallery toward Kit's room, wondered if she was in there with Kendrick. Not that it mattered. One night with a woman did not make him possessive at all. And it was pretty obvious that afternoon that she found Kendrick interesting.

He turned and walked the other way, toward St. Peter Street. The doors to the other rooms were all closed. He looked up and down St. Peter and found it dark. He stared down at Bourbon Street again. Just across the way a woman stood in an open doorway—she was naked, blonde, with pale skin and very large breasts. She was standing in the doorway, posed, hipshot, as an advertisement for the place. A damned good advertisement, too, he thought. At that moment she tilted her head up, saw him standing on the gallery. She smiled at him, and took a deep breath, which thrust her breasts out. She looked as if she might wave at him when he heard the scream.

He turned and ran back in the direction of his room. The scream had come from somewhere close. Could have come from somewhere on Bourbon Street, but he didn't think so. He kept going, past his room, until he got to the doors of Kit's room. They were open, the gauzy curtains blowing a bit in the breeze.

"Kit?"

No answer?

"Kit, are you there?"

Still no answer.

He went inside. If the layout of the room was the same as his there should have been a lamp on a table . . . There it was. He took out a match, lit the lamp, and turned it up. She was there, on the bed, with blood all around her. Her throat had been cut—and recently. Like just after the scream.

Clint waited in his room while the police removed Kit from hers. He'd gone downstairs to the lobby after finding Kit and told the desk clerk to send for the police. When they arrived they stuck him in his room and told him to stay there. Somebody would be along to talk to him—eventually.

There was a decanter of brandy in the room. He would have liked something stronger—or just a beer—but he'd have to make do with the brandy. He was drinking a second glass when there was a knock on the door, and it opened.

The man who stepped in was wearing a brown suit

and a matching bowler. He was tall, slender, in his forties, with a strong jaw and intelligent eyes.

"Mr. Adams?"

"That's right."

"I'm Inspector Devlin."

"Devlin?"

"Yes," the man said, "I'm the only Irish policeman on the New Orleans force. I've heard all about it many times already."

"Sorry."

"No problem. Can we talk?"

"Sure."

"That brandy?"

"Would you like a glass?"

"Please. I don't like seein' beautiful women cut up like that."

"See it a lot?" Clint asked, handing the man a glass.

"Mostly whores," the inspector said. "Never respectable women like Miss Devereaux."

"Did you know her?"

"I know who she is," Devlin said, "but I never met her. You?"

"We just met yesterday," Clint said. "We're both here to be judges for the contest out at the Fairgrounds."

"The Louisiana Shoot-out, right?"

"Yes."

"How well did you know her?"

Clint shrugged.

"As well as you can know someone you only met a day ago," he said. "We had a drink together. Oh, and I met her father."

"Father?"

"Fella named Baptiste."

"From Baptiste's, the bar?"

"That's the one."

"I know Baptiste," he said, "but I didn't know Kit was his daughter."

"I guess they don't—didn't—spread that around."

"I guess I'll have to let him know," Devlin said. He finished the brandy and put the glass down. "Now, can you tell me exactly what you heard and saw?"

Clint filled the inspector in as completely as he could.

"So you didn't see anyone runnin' from the room?" Devlin asked.

"No."

"And nothin' in the room?"

"Just the girl."

"You don't carry a knife, do you, Mr. Adams?" the inspector asked.

"Not as a rule, no."

"And you were at the other end of the gallery when you heard the scream?"

"That's right."

"Any witnesses to place you there?"

"Witnesses? Am I a suspect?"

"Everybody's a suspect, Mr. Adams," Devlin said. "I know who you are, and I know your reputation. This doesn't seem like the kind of thing you'd do, but I wouldn't be doing my job if I didn't ask."

"No, I guess not," Clint said. "Well, I was standing out there alone."

"Anybody see you? Maybe from one of the other rooms?"

"They were all dark."

"Well . . . guess I can't take you off my list—"

"Wait a minute," Clint said. "Across the street, across Bourbon, on the corner of St. Peter, there was a woman standing in a doorway."

"A woman."

"A naked woman."

"Oh," Devlin said, "that doorway. Who was the woman?"

"I don't know," Clint said, "but she was blonde and very . . . well, very naked."

Devlin scratched his head.

"I know the place," Devlin said. "You care to take a walk over there with me? If we can find her, and she recalls seein' you, I can take you off my list."

"Well," Clint said, "I'd know her if I saw her again. I guess I'll have to hope she'll know me."

"We can go and get that done right now," the inspector said.

"Well, then," Clint responded, "lead the way, Inspector."

TWENTY-ONE

They left the hotel, hit Bourbon Street, and turned right.

"Have you been to New Orleans before, Mr. Adams?" Devlin asked.

"Yes," Clint said, "and I've been to the Quarter before."

"Have you been to any of these clubs?"

"No," Clint said. "I usually find my female companionship in . . . other places."

"Sounds like a good idea," Devlin said.

"There," Clint said. "That's the doorway where I saw the woman."

They crossed the street. The door was still open, but now the doorway was empty. As Devlin and Clint approached, a huge black man with a gleaming bald head filled it, blocking the way.

"Inspector Devlin," the man said. His voice was very deep, came rolling out of him.

"Moses," Devlin said. "I'd like to come inside."

"You got a warrant?"

"I don't need one."

"Is this a raid?"

"No."

"You swear?"

"I swear, Moses," Devlin said. "No raid."

"Swear on the soul of Marie Laveau?" Moses asked.

"I swear, Moses."

"Who's this?"

"His name is Clint Adams," Devlin said. "He's staying at the hotel across the street, where a woman had her throat cut tonight."

"What's that got to do with me?"

"Nothin'," Devlin said, "I hope. But we need to see one of your girls."

"Which one?"

"I don't know," Devlin said. "Mr. Adams says he'll know her when he sees her."

"A big beautiful blonde," Clint said. "She was standing in the doorway a little while ago . . . naked."

"Naked in the doorway?" Moses asked. "Our girls ain't allowed to do that. I might have to fire her."

"Don't do that, Moses," Devlin said. "We just need to talk to her."

Moses thought it over, then said, "Okay. Come on inside."

He backed up to let them step inside. By now the women had been warned and were wearing flimsy garments. There were men there, too, all nervous looking.

"Stay here," Moses said. "I'll get the girl."

"You know who it is?" Devlin asked.

"I got an idea."

He moved into the dimness of the place.

"Moses owns this place," Devlin said. "He has a certain . . . arrangement with the local police."

"I see."

There was music playing from a piano they couldn't see. Presumably, it was farther in the room. Clint recognized it as music he could hear from his room.

Before long Moses returned with a blond woman in tow. Like the others, she was wearing a flimsy garment that did nothing to hide the bounty of her body. She had big breasts with hard nipples. Her robe was open in front and Clint could see the golden tangle of pubic hair between her thighs.

"Gents, this is Kasey."

"With a K," she said.

"Kasey what?"

She looked at Moses, who nodded.

"Winston."

"Miss Winston, were you standing in the doorway earlier this evening?"

Again she looked at Moses.

"Talk to the man."

"I, uh, stuck my head out the door to get some fresh air," she admitted.

"Do you know this man?" Devlin asked.

"Should I?"

She looked at Clint, a bemused smile on her pretty face.

"He ain't been in here tonight, if that's what you're askin'," she said. "I'd remember."

"So you've never seen him?"

"I told you, he ain't—hey, wait," she said, smiling suddenly. "You the fella up on the gallery across the street?"

"That's me."

"Then you know him?" Devlin confirmed.

"I saw him up on the gallery," she said. "Me and him, we had . . . a moment."

"And you recognize him from across the street?"

"I got really good eyes, mister," she said. "He was starin' at me and I caught him. He was there until . . . the scream. Somebody screamed, right? Is that what this is about?"

"A woman was killed in the hotel," Devlin said.

"Well, he didn't do it, if that's what you're thinkin'," she said. "He was makin' eyes at me when we heard the scream."

"Okay, Miss Winston," Devlin said. "That's all we need."

"Thank you, Kasey," Clint said.

"Any time," she said. "Stop back and see me. Buy me a drink to say thanks."

"I'll do that."

"Back to work, girl," Moses said, slapping Kasey on her meaty rump.

Then he looked at Devlin and Clint.

"You fellas done?"

"We're done, Moses," Devlin said. "Thanks for your cooperation."

"Thank you," Clint said.

He and Devlin stepped outside.

"So?" Clint asked. "Am I off your list of suspects?"

"You're off," Devlin said. "You should be glad that girl's got such good eyes."

"Among other good things," Clint said.

TWENTY-TWO

Devlin left Clint in front of his hotel.

"If you think of anything else," the inspector told him, "our office is right on Royal Street, just a couple of blocks away.

"I'll remember."

"Thanks for your cooperation."

As the inspector started to walk away, Clint almost called out to him. He felt bad not telling the man about Dave Kendrick, but he really didn't know if Kit and Kendrick had been together after they left the Fairgrounds.

What he had to do was talk to Kendrick himself, first.

He went back to his room, undressed, and got into bed. The sheets had been changed, so there was no hint of Kit left in the bed, but he still tossed and turned for a while before finally falling asleep.

In the morning he went down the street and found a small café to have breakfast in. Last night he had given the inspector the names of the two organizers—Cole Weston and Ed Cory. He wondered if they had been informed yet about the death of one of their judges.

When he got to the Fairgrounds, he saw that Jack Vermillion was already there, as were Cory and Weston.

"Where's Kit?" Cory asked. "We wanna get started as soon as we can."

That answered Clint's question. None of the three men had heard the news.

"I've got some bad news," he told them. "Kit was killed last night."

"What?" Weston said.

"How?" Vermillion asked.

"Great," Cory said. "Now we're short a judge."

The others all glared at him.

"Yeah, yeah," he added, "it's terrible. What happened?"

"Somebody cut her throat in her room," Clint said.

"Somebody?" Weston asked. "Who?"

"How did you find out?" Vermillion asked.

"I was out on the gallery when it happened. I heard her scream. By the time I got to her room, she was dead and the killer was gone."

"What did you do?" Cory asked.

"I sent for the police."

"Did you mention us?" Cory asked. "I mean, the Shoot-out?"

"You afraid of bad publicity?" Clint asked.

"Naw—well, yeah, but any publicity would probably be good."

"Ed . . ." Weston said.

"What? We're all thinkin' it. Hell, I'm gonna go see when we can get started. We probably only need two judges, anyway."

He turned and walked away.

"He's got a lot invested in this competition," Weston said by way of apology.

"I suspect the police will be here sometime today," Clint said.

"What for?" Vermillion asked.

"They're going to investigate Kit's murder," Clint said. "I talked to an inspector named Devlin."

"Devlin?" Weston said.

"You know him?"

"I've heard of him," Weston said.

"Well, he's the one looking into it."

"Did they suspect you?" Vermillion asked.

"They might have, but I had a witness who placed me out on the gallery when she screamed."

"Lucky for you, then," Vermillion said.

"Are you okay to judge today?" Weston asked Clint. "I mean, after all, we have a responsibility—"

"Don't worry, you can go on with your contests," Clint said. "Just be ready to talk to the police when they show up."

"Okay," Weston said. "We've got to finish up the moving target portion of the rifle shoot."

"Glass balls?" Vermillion asked.

"Too expensive," Weston said. "We used a ton of them yesterday. No, we got some clay plates."

"What?"

"Round plates made out of clay," Weston said. "They

shatter real good when you hit them. Somebody throws them in the air."

Vermillion looked at Clint, who shrugged.

"I don't care what they shoot at," Clint said. "Let's just get it over with."

Weston moved off to join his partner in getting things under way. Clint grabbed Vermillion's arm to hold him back.

"Have you seen Kendrick?"

"Yeah, he's here. Why?"

"I was wondering if he was with Kit last night," Clint said. "She seemed interested in him yesterday."

"Jealous?"

"Curious," Clint said. "You said Kendrick's a professional killer."

"I said professional gunman," Vermillion said. "He wouldn't kill unless there was profit in it for him. Where's the profit in killing Kit?"

"I don't know," Clint said. "I guess I'm going to have to ask him."

"You accuse him of murder, you better be able to back it up," Vermillion said.

"I'm not going to accuse him," Clint said. "I'm just going to ask him."

"He might not see the difference," Vermillion said. "You want me to back your play?"

"No," Clint said, "that would make it seem like I really was making a play. No, I'll just pull him aside sometime today and ask him."

"Maybe the police will beat you to it."

"That's possible," Clint said, wondering when Inspector Devlin would appear. "That's just possible."

TWENTY-THREE

Clint didn't have to wait long for his opportunity to talk to Dave Kendrick. Apparently, the professional gunman was not as good with a rifle as he was with a pistol, and he was soon out of the contest.

"I'll be right back," Clint said to Vermillion.

"Be careful."

Clint nodded, walked over to where Kendrick was standing.

"Tough luck," he said.

Kendrick looked at him, hesitated a moment before answering.

"Not so tough," he said. "I'm better with a handgun."

"I saw that yesterday," Clint said. "Did you hear the news?"

"What news?"

"Kit Devereaux."

"What about her?"

"She's dead."

Kendrick turned to face Clint.

"What?"

"I found her in her room," Clint said. "Somebody cut her throat."

"When?"

"Last night."

Kendrick turned back to face the shooters again.

"Why are you tellin' me?"

"I had the feelin' that you left with her yesterday," Clint said.

"What if I did?"

"I was just wondering if you were in her room last night."

"What if I was?" Kendrick asked. "You askin' me if I killed her?"

"Why would I ask you that?" Clint said. "Even if I did, you wouldn't tell me if you did it."

"Well, I didn't."

"Well, the police might be asking you the same question."

"Police?" Kendrick faced Clint again. "Why?"

"They're investigating her death," Clint said. "They'll probably talk to everyone here."

"Did you give them my name?"

"No," Clint said, "but I know the policeman I talked to will be out here sometime today."

Kendrick suddenly looked as if he wanted to bolt.

"If you give them my name, I ain't gonna take too kindly to it."

"Are you threatening me, Kendrick?"

"I know who you are, Adams," Kendrick said, "and I ain't scared of you."

"I never thought you were," Clint said. "If the police hear your name, it won't be from me. Good enough?"

Kendrick hesitated, then said, "Good enough."

Clint nodded, turned, and walked back to the judges' table.

"How'd it go?" Vermillion asked.

"He wouldn't say if he was with her or not," Clint said.

"Whataya think?"

"I don't know," Clint said. "I think I'll have to leave it up to the police to find out."

"You gonna give them his name?"

"I told him I wouldn't," Clint said. "They're bound to find out on their own."

"Sounds like a good idea," Vermillion said. "Let them do their job. Meanwhile, we got to do ours."

"Yeah," Clint said, looking out at the shooters. "Who's left?"

They finished with the rifle shoot and as they were setting up for the next round of shooting, Inspector Devlin showed up with a couple of men. He came marching right over to Clint.

"Good morning," he said. "Can you point me to the organizers of this competition?"

"I'll do better than that," Clint said. "I'll introduce you. Come on."

He didn't introduce Devlin to Vermillion, a slight that Texas Jack did not mind.

"Gents," Clint said, approaching Weston and Cory, "meet Inspector Devlin of the New Orleans police. Inspector, Ed Cory and Cole Weston."

"I'm happy to meet both of you," Devlin said. "I wish it was under other circumstances."

"Is this about Kit Devereaux?" Cory asked.

"Yes, it—"

"I don't know anything about that," Cory said. "Now, if you'll excuse me I've got to set up—"

"Hold on, Mr. . . . Cory, is it?"

"That's right. Ed Cory."

"I'm afraid I can't let you just walk away, sir."

"But I told you I don't know anything."

"I'm afraid I'll have to ask some questions, anyway," Devlin insisted.

"Inspector—"

"And I think I'd like to start with you, Mr. Cory, and then you, Mr. Weston."

"Of course, Inspector," Weston said. "We'll be happy to cooperate."

"I'm glad to hear that, sir. Meanwhile, my men will circulate and talk to some of the other people here."

"Is that really necessary, Inspector?" Ed Cory demanded.

"This is a murder investigation, sir," Devlin said, "I'm afraid it is."

"Well, fine then," Cory said. "Let's get it over with."

Devlin turned to Clint.

"Thank you, Mr. Adams. I won't be needing your help from here on in."

"That's fine with me, Inspector," Clint said.

"That is," Devlin added, "unless you have something else to tell me."

"No," Clint said, "I have nothing to add."

"Very well, then." Devlin turned to Ed Cory. "Mr. Cory, if you would join me over here?"

He walked Cory away from his partner.

"Clint," Weston said, "you have to find out who killed Kit."

"What? Why me?"

"Because you know how important this competition is," Weston said.

"I'm sorry, Cole," Clint said, "but measured up against a woman's life, this competition doesn't seem very important, at all."

In fact, Clint thought that no matter what you measured it against, the competition would come up lacking. To his way of thinking, this wasn't very important at all. But then, he didn't have as much invested in it as Cory and Weston did.

In fact, he had nothing invested at all.

"I don't think so, Cole."

"Don't you want to know who killed her?"

"Of course, I do," Clint said. "But it's the inspector's job to find out, not mine. I'm only here to be a judge, Cole, not a detective."

TWENTY-FOUR

Despite what he told Weston, Clint had every intention of finding out who had killed Kit. After all, she'd been murdered just a few feet from where he'd been standing. Also, after a night in bed with a beautiful woman he had to at least consider her a friend.

Clint went back to Vermillion and said, "I think I'm done."

"What?"

"This contest is a farce," he said. "I can't even take it seriously. And now with Kit being murdered I can't, in all good conscience, sit here and watch these people shoot at targets."

"You're gonna leave me alone with . . . them?" Vermillion asked.

"If you're going to keep judging, I'm sure they'll get someone to sit with you," Clint said. "Or you can walk away, too."

"I can't."

"Why not?"

"They're payin' my way."

"I could help, there."

"Naw," Texas Jack said. "You go ahead and walk away, Clint. Find the girl's killer. I'll hang around here awhile, see how it turns out. Maybe Kendrick will win. That'd be interestin'."

"I think Kendrick is liable to walk away, too."

"Yeah, you're right," Vermillion said. "He wouldn't want to talk to the law."

"Somebody's going to tell the inspector they saw Kendrick with Kit," Clint said. "My guess is he'll be gone before they can find him to question him."

"That might make them believe he killed her," Vermillion said. "They'll spend all their time looking for him."

"I had that thought, too."

"Do you think he did it?"

"I didn't notice him carrying a knife," Clint said, "and professional gunmen usually use guns to do their killing. So, no, I don't think he did it."

"Well," Vermillion said. "Why don't you go and do what you have to do to find out who did kill her. And if you tell me you need my help, I'll walk away from this mess in a second."

"I'll keep that in mind," Clint said.

Clint found Cole Weston and told him what his decision was.

"But you can't—"

"I can, and I am, Cole," Clint said. "Finding Kit's killer is more important than being a judge for your competition."

"But . . . you said that was the inspector's job."

"It is his job . . . but I'm going to try to do it, anyway."

"Well, couldn't you judge during the day and investigate in the evenings?"

Clint just stared at him.

"Never mind," Weston said. "It sounded stupid even to me when I heard it coming out of my mouth."

"Will you explain to your partner?"

"I will," he said, "but we won't be able to cover your expenses if you're not a judge."

"I understand that."

"And what's Texas Jack gonna do?"

"He's staying," Clint said, "so you have one judge left. I suggested one of you step in and judge with him."

"That's a way to go, yes," Weston said. "All right. I'll tell Ed."

"I'm sorry, Cole."

"No," Cole said, "you have to do what you have to do. I understand."

Clint looked around, saw the inspector and his men conducting interviews.

"Has the inspector talked to you yet?"

"Yes, he questioned Ed and then me."

"What did you tell him?"

"Not much," Weston said, then added, "oh, I did tell him that Dave Kendrick and Kit seemed to be gettin' a little . . . friendly yesterday."

"I was afraid someone would tell him that."

"Why? Was that wrong?"

"No, it's what you saw, so it isn't wrong," Clint said. "But I don't think Kendrick did it."

"Well, the police will question him."

"Have you seen him around since the police arrived?" Clint asked.

"Come to think of it, no."

"Then it's as I thought. He lit out when they got here."

"Then that means he did it?"

"No, it means the police are going to think he did it. And that means they won't be looking anywhere else."

"But you will."

"Yes," Clint said, "that's exactly where I'm going to look—elsewhere."

TWENTY-FIVE

Clint walked into Baptiste's, saw the big black man behind the bar with a rag tossed over one shoulder.

"Mr. Adams," Baptiste said, "how nice to see you again."

Clint didn't know if the police had been there yet, if Baptiste knew that his daughter was dead.

"Hello, Baptiste."

"If you're looking for my daughter I haven't seen her since she was here with you."

So he didn't know.

Clint leaned on the bar.

"Baptiste, I have some bad news."

Baptiste stiffened.

"She's dead," he said.

"How do you know?" Clint asked.

"I felt it," the older man said. "Last night. It happened last night, right?"

"Yes."

"I felt it, me."

"I'm sorry."

"How did it happen?"

Clint explained what he'd heard and what he saw when he found her.

"So you don't know who killed her?"

"No," Clint said. "The police are working on it, but I think they're going to end up going after the wrong man."

"So you will seek the right man?"

"Yes."

"Why?"

"Because I liked your daughter."

"You and my daughter . . . did you fornicate?" Baptiste asked.

"No," Clint answered. It was instinctive, when talking with a woman's father.

Baptiste studied him for a moment.

"She was like her mother, you know," Baptiste said. "Sinful . . . a whore at heart . . . but I loved her. I loved them both. That was my curse."

"Baptiste," Clint said, "do you know anyone who might have wanted to kill your daughter?"

"No."

"No? No men she rejected? No women whose men she stole?"

"I don't know these things, me."

"She told me she had just come back to town," Clint asked. "Where had she been?"

"She never left Louisiana," he said. "She might've been in the bayou. Or she might've gone to Baton Rouge."

"Did she have friends or family there?"

"Family in the bayou," Baptiste said. "I don't know about Baton Rouge. I just know she liked to go there— usually just to get away from here."

"But she never left Louisiana?"

"Never."

"All right," Clint said. "I'm down the street at the King Louis. If you think of anything helpful, please let me know."

"What about this contest you and Katherine were judging?"

"I've given that up so I can try to find Kit's killer."

"You feel that strongly about her death?"

"Yes," Clint said, "I feel that strongly about her death."

"Then I hope the spirit of Marie Laveau will be with you."

"Thank you, Baptiste."

Clint knocked on the locked door of the club he and Devlin had visited the night before. He waited, then pounded on the door again. When it finally opened the big black man, Moses, once again filled the whole doorway.

"We ain't open yet."

"Moses, remember me?" Clint asked. "I was here last night with Inspector Devlin."

Moses leaned out to take a better look at Clint. The sunlight reflected off his bald head.

"Oh, yeah, from the hotel across the street," he said. "We're still closed."

"I wanted to buy Kasey a drink."

"Well, you could do that if you came back tonight," Moses said, "but you have to be a member to get in."

"A member?"

"That's why we call it a club," Moses said. "We ain't a saloon, or a café, or a restaurant. We're a club."

"How do I become a member?"

"Like I said," Moses replied, "come back tonight after six. You can join, and then you can do whatever you want to Kasey."

"I just want to buy her a thank-you drink."

"Right."

Moses backed up and slammed the door in Clint's face.

TWENTY-SIX

Clint went back to the hotel to question the desk clerk and the cleaning staff. They all claimed to have seen nothing the night before, and not to have heard Kit scream. Clint couldn't question the second. He'd heard the scream because he was out on the gallery. But how could the desk clerk not have seen anything?

Clint decided to talk to the manager, Tate.

"Please, sir, have a seat," Tate said as Clint entered his office. "I hope there are no problems."

"Well, yeah," Clint said, "there's a big problem. Somebody was murdered in your hotel."

"Yes, of course," Tate said. "Shocking."

"What's shocking," Clint said, "is that someone got up to Miss Devereaux's room, cut her throat, and got away, apparently without your staff seeing anything."

"Well . . . yes . . ."

"Have the police been here to question your people yet?"

"Um, no, not yet."

"Well, they will be here soon," Clint said. "I think you should talk to your desk clerk about last night. In fact, I think we should do it right now."

"I'm sorry, Mr. Adams, but what is your interest in this?"

"I found the body, man!" Clint said. "Do you think I need some other reason to be outraged by this?"

"No, no, of course not."

Clint did something he never did. He hated doing it!

"Do you know who I am?"

"Well, um, yes sir—"

"Get your clerk up here and let's see what he has to say for himself."

"Um, the clerk on duty now was not on duty last night, sir."

"Well, where is the man who was on duty last night?"

"I suppose he's at home."

"Give me his address."

"I can't do—"

Clint stood up and slammed his hand down on the desk. Tate jumped and drew back.

"Give me the address."

"Yes, sir," Tate said. "R-right away."

TWENTY-SEVEN

The clerk's address was on Magazine Street. It was a long walk from the hotel, or a short hansom cab ride. Clint chose to take a cab, catching one right in front of the hotel.

When he reached the building, he saw it was a two-story wooden structure with a hardware store downstairs and rooms for rent upstairs. There was a stairway on the side that he took to the second floor. The door was unlocked. Clint went in and walked down the hall past the doors with the numbers one and two on them. Tate said the desk clerk, whose name was Jerry Heath, was in room three.

When he reached room three, he knocked. Tate said the man slept during the day and worked the night shift at the hotel. Clint knocked again, then pounded. As he pounded, the cheap lock sprung and the door snapped open.

"Jerry?" he shouted, pushing the door open.

The smell hit him right away, the metallic smell of blood, which he could also taste. He drew his gun and stepped into the room. Immediately he saw the man on the bloody bed, lying there with his throat cut.

"Damn it!"

It took a while for the police to find Inspector Devlin, even though Clint was the one who told them he was out at the Fairgrounds. Meanwhile they kept Clint waiting in the hallway. They also knocked on the other two doors, but got no answers. Clint hoped they wouldn't find two more occupants with their throats cut.

When Devlin arrived, he said, "You seem to have a habit of finding bodies."

"You would've found this one sooner or later," Clint said. "I just saved you the trouble."

"Oh, believe me," Devlin said, "this is still trouble."

"I couldn't get your men here to force open the other doors."

"Why should they?"

"I figure the same person who killed Kit Devereaux also killed the desk clerk, because he probably saw something. What if, while he was here killing the clerk, he thought someone in the other rooms might have seen or heard something?"

Devlin turned and barked at his men, "Force those other two doors."

"Yes, sir."

They forced them and found the rooms empty, which caused Devlin to give Clint the eye.

"Hey, they could've been dead in there."

"Yeah," Devlin said. "Come in here with me."

They reentered the room and looked at the body on the bed.

"His throat's been cut, like Kit's," Clint said.

"I can see that," Devlin said.

"You manage to find anything out today?"

"I heard from some people about a guy named Kendrick," Devlin said. "Dave Kendrick. Know him?"

"I met him."

"What do you know about him and the Devereaux girl?" the policeman asked.

"They met yesterday, I think," Clint said. "Beyond that I don't know anything."

"Did you know he's a professional gunman?"

"Yes."

"Do you think he killed her?"

"No."

"Neither do I."

"Really?"

Devlin looked at him.

"Did you think I'd jump at the easiest solution?" he asked.

"To be truthful? Yes."

"Well, I figure a professional gunman will usually use a gun to kill somebody," Devlin said. "Now we have two dead bodies with their throats cut. So I figure I'm lookin' for a killer who uses a knife."

"Got any suspects?"

"We have a few in town who specialize in knives, but I don't have anybody with a motive yet."

"What about somebody working for hire?"

"I still have to have a motive," Devlin said. "You spent some time talking to Miss Devereaux, didn't you?"

"Yes."

"Let's go outside." Devlin turned to his men and gestured to the body. "Get him out of here."

"Yes, sir."

They stepped back into the hall, and then Devlin led the way outside and down the steps.

"Did she say anything to you at any time about being afraid of anyone?"

"No," Clint said. "She didn't strike me as the kind of woman who was afraid."

"No problems with men?"

"No," Clint said, "but we only spent a short time together. I think you need to talk to someone who knew her better."

"Like who?"

"Her father, I guess."

"Ah, Baptiste," Devlin said. "Yes, I intend to talk with him."

"Maybe he can tell you who her friends were," Clint said.

"How well do you know him?"

"Not at all," Clint said. "I only met him after I met her."

"Okay," Devlin said, "now tell me what you were doing here."

"Looking for this desk clerk," Clint said. "I wanted to talk to him about last night, find out if he saw anything."

"That's my job, Mr. Adams."

"I may have known Kit Devereaux a short time," Clint said, "but I considered her my friend. I don't like it when my friends are killed."

"I'm aware of your reputation, Mr. Adams," Devlin said. "What are your plans if you happen to find this killer before I do?"

"I haven't thought that far ahead, Inspector," Clint said. "If I come face to face with him, I'll make the decision at that time."

"My advice would be to turn him over to me."

"You're not going to tell me to stay away? Mind my own business? Stay out of your way?"

"I'd like to tell you all of that," Devlin said, "but I have a feeling it would do me no good."

Clint didn't say anything.

"So," Devlin continued, "remember where I am, on Royal Street. If I'm not there, someone will know where to find me."

"All right."

"One warning."

"What's that?"

"If you find this man and kill him," Devlin said, "make damned sure you can prove self-defense to my satisfaction."

"I'll certainly keep that warning in mind, Inspector," Clint promised.

TWENTY-EIGHT

Clint left the police to their job and took a hansom cab back to his hotel. As he entered, the manager, Tate, came running over to him.

"Mr. Adams, were you able to speak with—"

"He's dead."

Tate stepped back as if he had been slapped.

"What?"

"You're going to need to get yourself a new night man," Clint said.

"But . . . how?"

"His throat was cut, just like Miss Devereaux's."

"But why?"

"Apparently," Clint said, "he saw or heard something, and the killer knew it."

"My God," Tate said. "This is . . . shocking."

"No more shocking than Miss Devereaux's murder," Clint said.

"With all due respect, sir," Tate said, "I did not personally know Miss Devereaux."

Clint hesitated a moment, then realized the man was absolutely right to react the way he was reacting.

"You're right, Tate," he said. "My condolences on the loss of your man, and my apologies for being insensitive."

Now Tate looked shocked.

"Well . . . thank you, sir."

"Please pass the word to the rest of your staff to contact me if they think they heard or saw anything. If they did, they might be in danger."

"Oh . . . of course." Tate looked as if he hadn't considered that.

"You didn't see or hear anything, did you, Tate?" Clint asked.

"Me? No, no, of course not. I—I wasn't even on the premises last night."

"I see," Clint said. "Well, pass the word."

"I will," Tate said. "I certainly will."

Clint left the man to his grief and went up to his room. He immediately stepped out onto the gallery and leaned on the rail, staring down at Bourbon Street. His trip to New Orleans certainly was not going the way he had hoped.

The competition, the so-called Louisiana Shoot-out, seemed a farce for something that had supposedly been planned well. Weston and Cory did not seem to know what they were doing. It made Clint wonder why he, and maybe even why Texas Jack, had been invited.

He walked to the Toulouse Street end of the gallery, where Kit's room had been. The doors were closed. He tried them, found them locked, but from the looks of them they would not have been hard to open. He peered through the glass, saw that the bloody sheets had been removed from the bed, but that the bare mattress was still stained. He wondered if Tate was going to have the mattress replaced. He hoped so, for the benefit of the next guest.

He turned and walked to the St. Peter side of the gallery. He looked down at the private club owned by the big black man, Moses. Saw that the front door was closed. He didn't know if that meant they were still closed or not. Moses had told him to come back after six. Was that when they opened, or was that when Kasey would be there?

He turned and went back to his room. Now that he had given up on judging the Shoot-out, he didn't know quite what to do with himself. Maybe he should have fulfilled his obligation, but the whole thing still felt wrong to him, like there was something else going on. Also, why would someone like Dave Kendrick be entered? And where was Kendrick now?

Clint approached the closed door of the club at six fifteen. He knocked and waited. When the door opened, Moses appeared.

"You're back."

"Yes."

"Still want to join?"

"Yes."

"Come in, then."

Moses backed up and Clint entered. The big black man closed the door again.

"No open-door advertisement tonight?" Clint asked.

"We don't do that a lot. You gotta pay a hundred dollars to join for a year."

"I'm not going to be here for a year," Clint said. "There's no cheaper membership?"

"Six months?"

"How about a week?"

They continued to negotiate and finally settled on a one-month membership. Clint paid the man in cash.

"Okay," he said, "so now I'm a member, right?"

"Yes."

"Is Kasey working tonight?"

"Yes, she's here."

"Good, then I'd like to see her."

"Go to the bar," Moses said. "I'll tell her you're here."

"The bar? Is that included in the membership?"

"No."

"What is?"

Moses glared at him and said, "You get to come in."

Clint was standing at the bar with a cold beer he had to admit was delicious when Kasey sidled up next to him. She was wearing another flimsy robe, but she might as well have been naked.

"You came back." She pressed one firm hip right up against him.

"You invited me."

"To buy me a drink, right?"

"That's right."

She called the bartender over and said, "Champagne, Joe."

Clint smiled.

"Why doesn't that surprise me?"

"I'm expensive," she said, "but then you've seen the goods, haven't you?"

"Well," Clint reminded her, "they were on display."

"They were supposed to be," she said. "That's my job. Are you still in trouble?"

"In trouble?"

"The murder across the street?"

"Oh, that," he said. "No, you helped me out there. Thanks again."

He raised his glass to her, and she followed. They both drank.

"Did you really hear her?" he asked.

"Hear her?"

"The scream," Clint said. "Did you really hear her scream?"

Kasey looked sheepish.

"No, not really," she said, "but I thought it would help you more if I said I did."

"Well," Clint said, "I suppose I owe you two drinks, then."

"I'll take them," she said, and signaled to the bartender again.

TWENTY-NINE

"You know," Kasey said, "I noticed you standing up on that gallery right away."

"You did?"

"I was posing there for you."

"Well, I saw you," he said, "and I appreciate it."

"Do you really want to stay in this place?" she asked.

"I'm only here to see you."

"I can pretty much make my own hours here," she said. "Moses knows I'm the most popular girl here."

"What's your point?"

"My point is . . . do you want to get out of here?" she asked.

"And go where?"

"Oh, I don't know," she said. "Your room?"

"I should tell you," he said, "I don't usually pay for a woman."

"That's okay," she said. "I haven't fucked anybody for free in a long time."

• • •

Kasey told Moses she was leaving, then walked across the street with Clint. For the walk to the hotel she had donned a simple dress, which clung to her body, leaving nothing to the imagination. The night clerk—a new man, of course—didn't give Clint a second look. His eyes were too busy following Kasey as they walked across the floor and then up the stairs. He couldn't take his eyes off her undulating buttocks until they were out of sight.

Clint opened the door and let Kasey go into the room first.

"You know," she said as he closed the door, "I've worked across the street from this hotel for a long time but I've never been in any of the rooms."

"Feel free to look around," he said.

She made a circuit of the room, then paused in front of the closed French doors.

"Go ahead," he said.

She opened the doors, stepped out, leaned on the railing, and looked down at Bourbon Street.

"I love this street," she said, "and this town. You wouldn't think so, considering what I do for a living."

He came out and stood beside her.

"Doesn't much matter what you do for a living," he said. "It's what you do with your life."

"You know, that's what I think, too."

They stared down at the street together for a few moments.

"There have been times when I've stood in that doorway and I've seen people having sex up here," she said.

"You can see into their rooms?"

"No, silly," she said, "I mean out here, on the gallery. They don't think anyone can see them up here when it's dark, but when the moon is high and bright like tonight, I can see them."

"Clearly?"

"Well, it depends on what they're doing, but yeah, sometimes."

"Like what?"

She turned her head to look at him.

"Whataya mean?"

"I mean what things could you see them doing?" he asked.

"Well . . . kissing."

"You mean, like this?"

He leaned over and kissed her lightly.

"No, not like that, not at all," she said, as if scolding him. "More like this."

She turned to him, put her arms around his neck, pressed her body against his, and kissed him deeply, opening her mouth hungrily.

When she broke the kiss, they were both breathless from it.

"Oh, like that."

"Yes."

"Anything else?"

"Well," she said, "you know you can see through this railing, so I've seen . . . other things."

"Like what?"

She laughed. "You want me to show you?"

"Yes."

"Right here?"

"Yes."

"It's not dark yet, you know," she warned. "Someone might see from the street."

He looked down at the people on Bourbon Street.

"They all seem to have their own business to tend to," he said.

"Okay, but I'm warning you, once we start I'm not gonna stop."

"That's okay."

"Are you sure?"

"Yes."

"No matter how far we go?"

He smiled.

"No matter."

"Okay, then."

THIRTY

"I saw a man and a woman out here once, months ago. She got to her knees in front of him, like this."

Kasey got down on her knees.

"Then she undid his pants."

She loosened his belt.

"Of course, that man wasn't wearing a gun."

Clint undid the gun belt. For a moment he considered hanging it over the rail, but it might have fallen over the side to the street below. Instead he reached out and hung it on the handle of the French doors.

That done, Kasey continued to undo his pants, pulling them down his legs so they pooled around his feet.

"Then she did this." She ran her hands up and down his thighs. "And this." She slid his underwear down, and his penis, already thickening, sprang into view.

"Oh," she said, "the other man wasn't this . . . big."

"You could see that from across the street?"

"I could tell by the way she held him."

She took his penis in both hands.

"She only used one hand," she explained.

"Oh . . ."

She slid her fingers up and down as he grew in her grip, then slid one hand down to cup his balls.

"Then she did this."

She leaned forward and took him into her mouth. He looked down at the street. People were walking beneath them, passing by, crossing the street, but no one was looking up.

She began to move her head, sliding him in and out of her mouth wetly. He'd wondered how far she would go, and she had already exceeded his expectations. Now he thought the sky was the limit.

"Didn't the man do anything to the woman?" he asked, thickly.

"Oh, yes," she said, letting him slide from her mouth, "but first the woman got naked."

"How naked?"

She stood with an amused look on her face, but she also looked excited. She slid her dress from her shoulders and let it drop to the floor. She wasn't wearing anything underneath. Her bare breasts were pale, with pink nipples; pear-shaped, almost pendulous. The hair between her legs was as golden as the hair on her head. Her hips were wide, thighs almost chunky. She did a slow turn so he could see her solid buttocks.

"Is this naked enough?" she asked

"I don't think so," he said when he was able to find his voice.

"What?"

"I don't think that other woman could have been this naked," he said. "I don't think any woman could be as naked as this."

"Well," she told him, "the man was more naked than you are."

She was challenging him.

He had to remove his boots before he could completely get rid of his pants and underwear. Then he straightened and removed his shirt.

Totally naked, he spread his arms and asked, "How's this?"

"That," she said, "is perfect."

"Then what happened?" he asked.

"Well," she said, "the man bent the woman over the railing . . . like this."

She leaned over the railing so that her big breasts were dangling, giving him a great view of her pale buttocks. "I think you can guess the rest, can't you?"

"I think I can manage that."

He moved up behind her, rubbed his erection up and down the crack between her ass cheeks. Then he slipped his right hand up between her thighs to use his fingers to get her wet. She moaned and leaned into his touch. Finally, he spread her legs, took hold of her hips, and slid his cock up and into her. She gasped, but began to lunge back against him even before he started moving his hips forward.

He could see the people across the street over her head, but they still were not looking up. As she gasped and he grunted, fucking deeply and for all they were worth, he looked across the street, where there was another hotel. He thought they were safe until he saw someone at the window of one of the rooms. It was a woman, and from what he could see of her she was pretty, with long dark hair. She pushed her curtains aside and stood fully in her window, staring at them. Her mouth formed an "O" and her eyes were wide. He was almost ready to grab Kasey and pull her back into the rooms when he realized what the woman in the window was doing. She had undone the buttons of her dress and, with one hand, she was rubbing her own breast. Her other hand was down below the window level. Both hands were busy, and he knew now that her mouth was not open in shock.

"Look," he said to Kasey.

"Where?" she grunted.

"Across the street, the window right across from us."

Kasey raised her head to look, saw the woman, and instantly knew what she was doing.

"Good for her," she laughed. "We should invite her over."

"I think," Clint said, "I have my hands full right now."

To illustrate his point he took two hands full of her butt and squeezed.

She laughed and waved to the woman across the street . . .

THIRTY-ONE

The time came when Kasey gripped the railing so tightly that it started to shake. As Clint continued to drive himself into her, he wondered if the railing would hold.

Finally, he felt her begin to tremble and then a high-pitched sound came from deep inside of her. He knew the people below them, and across from them, would hear it. They'd have to. And the woman across the way. She'd moved away from her window eventually, and had not returned. Maybe she was ashamed. Maybe not. Maybe she was just exhausted.

"Oh God," Kasey said, her legs trembling as waves of pleasure flowed over her.

She slumped, and he withdrew from her so he could lift her in his arms and carry her inside.

"That's enough of a show for everyone else," he told her, setting her down on the bed. "Now the show's just for us."

She smiled, held her arms out to him, and said, "Just for you."

He let her fold him into her arms and kissed her for a long time. Finally, he moved from her luscious mouth to her neck, her shoulders, and her beautiful big breasts with their hard pink nipples.

She shuddered as he sucked her nipples, holding his head there, moaning and laughing.

Finally, he left her nipples and continued down her body, over her belly to the golden triangle of hair. He pressed his face to her and probed with his tongue until she squealed and lifted her hips. He slid his hands beneath her buttocks to hold her up and continued to work on her with tongue and lips until her entire body shuddered again, went taut, and then slack.

"Oh God," she said. "Jesus, where did you learn to do that? You are so good at it!"

"Practice makes perfect."

"Practice?" she said, looking down at him. "You must have left a string of satisfied women behind you on your way here."

He moved to lie down next to her, his still-hard dick prodding at the air insistently.

"I haven't had any complaints," he said.

"And you're not gonna have any yourself, when I get through with you," she said, grabbing his cock.

She slid down his body, teased him with her tongue a bit before taking him into her hot mouth. She sucked him avidly, and there was no stopping her this time. She sucked him and caressed him until he had to lift his hips off the bed before exploding into her mouth—and she wasn't done there. Before he could soften, she mounted him and stuffed him inside the hot, steamy depths of her pussy. As she rode him, he grew fully hard again and, since this would be his second time, he lasted a lot longer before groaning and emptying himself into her.

She flopped down next to him, her golden flesh dappled with sweat, her breasts heaving as she tried to catch her breath.

"Well, you were right," he said, gasping for air himself. "I have no complaints."

She slid her hand down over his belly and said, "And the night ain't done yet."

The night was far from done because Clint wasn't ready to turn in yet. He asked Kasey if she wanted to go out and get something to eat.

"I have to go back to the club to change into something more . . . appropriate."

"I'm not planning anything fancy," he said. "In fact, you can pick the place."

"That's fine, but I still need to change," she said, leaping off the bed and hurriedly dressing. "I'll meet you in the lobby in an hour."

"An hour?" His stomach was grumbling.

"I can't just throw some clothes on," she said. "I want to look nice for you."

"All right," he sighed. "An hour it is."

She ran to the bed, kissed him soundly, then hurried out the door.

Clint reclined on the bed, his hands behind his head, staring out through the French doors at the moonlight. He was pleasantly fatigued, but felt just a little guilty about having sex with Kasey instead of being out trying to find out who killed Kit Devereaux. Her father had said that she spent some time in Baton Rouge. Maybe, he thought, he should take a ride there tomorrow and see what he could find out.

Tonight, however, was for eating, and for keeping Kasey to her word that "the night ain't done yet."

THIRTY-TWO

In a saloon on N. Rampart and Esplanade, Victor Newman and Anton DuBois were once again waiting for Ed
Cory to arrive. He had sent them each an urgent mes-
sage to meet him there. Before he arrived, however,
Dave Kendrick walked in and approached their table.

"Kendrick," Newman said. "I thought you were watching Clint Adams."

"Did you hear about the woman being murdered?"
Kendrick asked. "Katherine Devereaux?"

"Yes," DuBois answered. "That was unfortunate.
What's it got to do with you?"

"I was with her that night."

"What?"

"You didn't—" DuBois started.

"You finish that question and I'll put a bullet in ya,"
Kendrick said.

DuBois shut up.

"The police are lookin' for me," Kendrick said to
Newman. "I got to lie low."

"You have a job to do," Newman said. "Remain at the competition and watch Adams."

"That would be pretty hard, since Adams quit."

"He what?" Newman asked.

"Walked off," Kendrick said. "He figures to find out who killed the woman, thinks that's more important than some shoot-out."

"Goddamn it!" Newman swore.

That must have been why Cory had called this meeting.

"All right," Newman said. "What do you need?"

"Some money to get out of the city."

"Okay, but I need you to do something for me first."

"Like what?"

"I need another man, reliable with a gun," Newman said, "to take your place."

"I've got just the man."

"Have him meet me here tomorrow at noon."

"I don't know if I can get hold of him that fast," Kendrick said.

"You want the money to get out of town?"

"I'll get 'im."

"I thought so. Be here at noon with him and I'll give you the money. Meanwhile, stay out of sight."

"That's my plan."

Kendrick left and DuBois said, "Now what?"

"Now we wait for Cory."

Ed Cory arrived about half an hour later. He knew by the way the two men were looking at him that something was amiss.

"You already know," he said, sitting down.

"Kendrick was here," Newman said.

"You know, this all might be his fault," Cory said.

"How's that?" DuBois asked.

"If he killed that woman—"

"He didn't," Newman said.

"How do you know?" Cory asked.

"He told me," Newman said.

"And you believe him?"

"I do," Newman said. "I'm more inclined to blame you for the debacle."

"This . . . what? Blame me? Why?"

"You enlisted the woman as a judge," DuBois said.

"That wasn't me, that was Cole."

"You could have overruled him," Newman said.

"Look, this isn't a total loss," Cory said.

"How do you figure that?" Newman asked.

"Well, Adams is still in town, and Vermillion is still judging."

"The competition is still going?" Newman asked, surprised.

"Yes."

The two rich men exchanged a glance.

"Okay," Newman said, "we're getting a man to replace Kendrick. You keep track of Adams."

"How do I do that?"

"Figure it out," DuBois said.

"Use that partner of yours," Newman said. "He's the one who enlisted Adams."

"That's true."

Newman pointed his finger at Cory.

"Keep this thing together for two more days," Newman said. "That's all we need."

"Why two days?"

"Never mind," Newman said. "Don't ask questions, just do it."

"Well, okay, but—"

"Get out, Cory," Newman said. "We're done."

Cory looked insulted, but didn't have the nerve to say anything. He got up and left.

"Let's have something to eat," Newman said.

"Here?" DuBois looked appalled.

"Good God, no!" Newman said, shocked. "Let's go to Antoine's."

THIRTY-THREE

"I hope you don't mind," Kasey said to Clint, "but I've always wanted to eat here."

Clint looked at the front of Antoine's and knew this was going to cost him.

But the way Kasey had gotten dressed up, it would be worth it. She was wearing a red gown with lots of flesh showing. As they walked in, they attracted the eye of everyone in the place, men and women.

As they were shown to a table, Clint studied the other diners. There were other women in gowns, some of them even showing as much skin as Kasey was, only they didn't have the skin necessary to make the dress work.

The maître d' handed them each a menu and promised that a waiter would be over soon.

"Don't worry," Kasey said, leaning forward and taking his breath away with the view of her cleavage, "I won't break you."

"Order anything you like," he told her. "If you've always wanted to eat here, you might as well enjoy it."

"Really?"

"Yes, really."

"Wow," she said, "am I glad I gave you an alibi."

"That's not all I'm glad you gave me," he told her.

She looked around, then leaned forward again and lowered her voice.

"Am I dressed too trashy for this place?" she whispered.

"No trashier than anyone else," he said. "The women in this place wish they could look the way you do in that dress."

"My hair—I didn't have time to do more than comb it," she complained.

"Your hair looks beautiful," he said. "You look beautiful. Stop worrying and just enjoy yourself."

She sat back and smiled.

"You know," she said, "I think I'm gonna do just that."

When the waiter came over, Clint said, "We'll begin with a bottle of champagne."

"Yes, sir."

"French champagne," Kasey said.

"Yes, miss."

"And two steak dinners, all the trimmings," Clint said.

"With Cajun spices," Kasey added.

"Of course, miss," the waiter said.

"And hurry up with the champagne," Clint said.

"Coming right out, sir."

On the other side of the room Victor Newman and Anton DuBois were having dinner. Both had noticed the man come in with the blonde.

"Good God," DuBois said, "she's about to fall out of that dress."

"One can only hope, Anton," Newman said, and both men laughed. "Wait a minute, I know that woman."

"Do you?" DuBois asked.

"Yes, from a club I . . . frequent. What's she doing in here, eating among respectable people?"

"Do you know the man?" DuBois asked.

"I've never seen him before."

"I wonder who he is," DuBois said.

"Call the waiter over," Newman said. "Let's ask if he knows."

DuBois waved at the waiter, the same man who was waiting on Clint and Kasey. The man hurried over.

Clint and Kasey were working on the champagne when the dinner came. The pungent Cajun spices opened Clint's nostrils.

"I hope this won't be too hot for you, Clint," Kasey said.

Not too hot, Clint thought, but too well done. He generally liked his meat rare, but this was Cajun cooking, where things came blackened more times than not.

The waiter left the plates and then walked back to a table across the room.

"Did you ask him?" Newman inquired.

"I didn't have to, sir," the waiter said. "The woman called him Clint."

"All right," Newman said. "Thank you."

As the waiter moved away the two men stared at each other.

"Could it be?" DuBois asked.

"It's a hell of a coincidence either way," Newman said. "Either it's him, or another man named Clint."

THIRTY-FOUR

"We have to get out of here before he sees us," DuBois said.

"You have to relax," Newman said. "There's no way he would recognize us, especially not you."

"But—"

"Just eat your food, Anton," Newman said. "We'll wait for him to leave, and then we'll leave."

"Sit here the whole time?"

"We'll have dessert."

"Wow," Clint said, his eyes tearing from the spices.

"Good?"

"Very."

She looked around the dining room.

"Twice in one day," she said, shaking her head. "I have to pinch myself."

"About what?"

"First I get to see inside a hotel I've been looking at for months, and now this place," she said.

"You could eat in places like this more often, you know."

"Not on what I get paid."

"You're a beautiful woman, Kasey," Clint said. "There are any number of men who would like to take you to supper in places like this."

"Oh, I know that," she said. "At least in the club money changes hands honestly. I know what the men want, and they know what I'll do for money."

Clint sat back, waiting for his eyes to stop watering before he tried another piece of steak.

"You seem pretty smart, Kasey."

"In other words, what's a smart girl like me doing working in a club like Moses's?"

"Pretty much."

"Well, the Moses part is easy," she said. "He keeps his girls safe—and he keeps his best girl safer."

"I'll bet."

"And the club is better than the brothels, the cribs, or the street."

"I can understand that."

"You can? Good. I'd hate for you to look down on me for what I do."

"I'd never do that, Kasey," Clint said. "You have to do what you have to do to survive."

"And that's what you do?"

He leaned forward and picked up his fork.

"That's what we all do."

"Did you hear me?"

Clint looked across the table at her.

"What?"

"Where did you go?"

"Sorry," he said. "There are two men taking their time over a couple pieces of pie."

"And?"

"And they keep looking over here."

"At me?" she asked.

"I hope so."

"Oh, I see," she said. "If they recognized you . . . You have to be constantly alert, don't you?"

"Only if I want to stay alive."

"Well, you seem to have done a good job of that up to now."

"And I want to keep doing it," he said.

"Which two men?"

"It doesn't matter," he said. "They don't look like they're armed."

"And you obviously are."

"Always."

"What about places where you can't wear a holster?" she asked.

"I have another gun," he told her, "fits into my belt very nicely."

"I don't think I'd like to have to live that way," she said.

"Seems to me you have to be pretty alert in your work, as well."

"You have a point there," she said. "The wrong man can kill you. I guess we have that much in common."

"Yes, we do."

"What do you want to do about your two friends?" she asked.

He thought a moment, then laughed.

"What's so funny?"

"I think they're biding their time, waiting for us to leave."

"And?"

"I think we can make them wait a good long time," he answered.

"Shit!"

"What?" DuBois said.

"I just realized . . ."

"Just realized what?"

Newman pushed his coffee cup away. It clinked off his empty pie dish.

"He knows we're watching him."

"What makes you say that?"

"Because he's playing with us," Newman said, "making us wait before he gets up and leaves."

DuBois looked around the dining room. Other than their table and the one Clint Adams was sharing with the big-breasted blonde, there were only two other tables still occupied.

"What do we do?"

"We get out of here, right now."

"They're leaving," Clint said.

"Why?"

"They figured it out and are tired of waiting."

"And what do we do?"

"We'll wait until they're gone, and then I'll put you in a hansom cab home."

"Not back to our hotel?"

"No," Clint said, "not until I figure out what's going on."

"You could come home with me," she said.

His first instinct was to say no, but then he thought again.

"That," he said, "might really confuse things."

THIRTY-FIVE

Clint woke the next morning in Kasey's bed. The sunlight streaming in her window turned her entire naked body to gold. She was lying on her stomach, full breasts flattened beneath her. There was a small patch of downy hair on the small of her back, glinting in the sunlight. He felt his cock swelling. He put his hand on her buttocks, slid his middle finger along the crease between them.

She moaned, moved her legs, rubbed her crotch inside the sheet as he massaged her butt.

"I like having you in my bed," she said. "I've never had a man here before."

"Never?"

"I'd never bring anyone from the club here."

"What about . . . a boyfriend?"

"Who has time for that?" she asked. "I'm trying to make as much money as I can so I can get out of the club."

"And then what?"

"And then I leave New Orleans."

"I thought you loved it here?"

"I do," she said, "but I've heard that New Orleans—specifically the French Quarter—is the only European city in America. I mean to see more European cities."

He slid his hand between her thighs, found her slick and wet.

"But not this morning?"

She wiggled her butt as his fingers delved into her, and then she turned over.

"No," she said with a grin, "not this morning."

Clint left an exhausted Kasey in her bed and headed back to his hotel. He thought about the two men in the restaurant the night before. They hadn't been armed, and were well dressed. They were the kind of men who, if they wanted to kill him, would hire it done.

The question was, why would they want him killed? He conjured up their faces and wasn't able to identify either of them.

Then he thought about Dave Kendrick. The only reason he could see for the man to have signed up for the shoot-out was if he'd been sent to do it. Suddenly, Clint thought he could put the three men together in his head. The only problem was, Kendrick was among the missing, probably either hiding from the police, or he'd left town altogether.

If either of those were true, and these men had hired him, then they'd have to replace him.

He went to his hotel, had a bath, put on some clean clothes, and then walked to the police station on Royal Street.

Clint was shown into Inspector Devlin's office. The man stood up and came around his desk, hand out.

"Nice to see you, Mr. Adams."

"Inspector."

They shook hands.

"Have a seat," Devlin invited. "What can I do for you? Or is this a case of what you can do for me?"

"I'm not sure," Clint said, sitting. "I just thought we'd talk."

"About what?" Devlin went back around his desk and sat down.

"Dave Kendrick."

"What about him?"

"You're looking for him, aren't you?"

"I am."

"He didn't do it."

"How do you know?"

"Because I spoke to him before he disappeared."

"How do you know he disappeared?"

"You can't find him, can you?"

"No."

"Well, he must have heard you were looking for him, figured him for the murder."

"But you don't."

"I told you," Clint said. "I spoke to him before he left. He had no reason to do it."

"Then who did?"

"I don't know."

"You can't tell me who did it," Devlin said, "but you can tell me who didn't?"

"That's right."

Devlin wiped his hand across his mouth.

"Is that all you came to tell me?"

"All I came to tell you, but not all I came to ask you."

"What do you mean?"

"I had supper at Antoine's last night," Clint said, "with a lady."

"That must've cost you a pretty penny."

"That's not the point," Clint said. "There were two men there who were very interested in me."

Clint went on to explain his theory, about the two men, about Kendrick.

"So you think these two men might have sent Kendrick to the contest to go after you? Isn't that a little far-fetched? I mean, based on what little evidence you have?"

"Unfortunately it's the way I have to think. I can't afford to wait for evidence like you can."

Devlin looked away.

"Sore spot?"

"Well, I was keying my investigation on Kendrick without any real evidence," Devlin admitted.

"So, you don't have to take my word that he didn't do it. Just keep investigating."

"I intend to," Devlin said. "That is my job. Is that why you came here? To remind me of my job?"

"No," Clint said, "I thought if I described these gentlemen to you, you might be able to tell me who they are."

"All right, go ahead."

Clint did so, hoping he had been observant enough. Even as he was describing them, he knew there was no use.

"Sorry," Devlin said, "that sounds like a lot of men in New Orleans—and many of them dine at Antoine's."

"I thought you might say that," Clint said, standing up. "Thanks anyway."

"I could give you the names of a few men they might use to replace him."

"I don't think they'd use locals," Clint said. "Probably bring somebody in."

"Of course, you have more experience with this than I do."

"Good luck finding Kit's killer," Clint said. "Have you talked to her father?"

"Baptiste? Yeah. He wasn't all that broken up about it, though."

"What?"

"Seemed to think she might have deserved what she got."

"Christ . . ."

"Don't worry," Devlin said. "I'm not going to quit."

"What about Baton Rouge?"

"What about it?"

"Baptiste told me she had friends there."

"He give you any names?"

"No."

"He didn't even tell us about that," Devlin said. "I'll see if I can get any names out of him."

"How about letting me do it?" Clint asked.

"Why?"

"I'd just like to be helpful, and maybe he'd talk to me easier than to the police."

"You might be right," Devlin said. "Okay, go ahead, but let me know what you find out."

"I'll be in touch," Clint said, and left.

THIRTY-SIX

Baptiste's was open for business, but not doing much of it at that early hour. In fact, there was only one customer at the moment, sitting alone at a table with a beer.

Baptiste was behind the bar.

"Back again?"

"I just have a few questions," Clint said.

"About what?"

"About your daughter's murder."

Baptiste just stared at him.

"Inspector Devlin told me you weren't too upset about Kit's death," Clint said. "He seems to think that you believe she may have deserved what she got."

The black man stared at him stoically.

"That can't be right, can it?"

"They all deserve what they get, don't they?" Baptiste asked.

"They all?" Clint asked. "Who are we talking about, Baptiste?"

The black man leaned forward and said, "Women."

Clint stared at the man for a few moments.

"All women deserve to be killed? Is that what you're saying?"

Stoic.

"Does that include Marie Laveau?"

Clint didn't see the big man move, but suddenly both of Baptiste's hands were around his throat. He tried to pry them loose, but he couldn't. He couldn't breathe and things were starting to darken around the edges of his vision. Finally, he did the only thing he could do. He drew his gun and pressed it to Baptiste's temple, then cocked the hammer.

Just as suddenly as they had appeared, the black man's hands dropped away and Clint took a deep breath.

"Good move, Baptiste," Clint said. "I would have blown your head off."

"You blaspheme."

"My question about Marie Laveau?"

Clint holstered his gun, touched his throat where Baptiste's powerful hands had been wrapped. If it happened again, he'd just draw and fire.

"Baptiste, I need to know about Baton Rouge."

"What about it?"

"Who were Kit's friends there?"

"Her name was Katherine."

"All right," Clint said. "Who were Katherine's friends?"

"I didn't know her friends," Baptiste said. "I only know she had friends there."

"Female friends?"

"I don't know."

"Are you sure?"

"I do not know my daughter's friends, especially not if they were men."

"Baptiste," I asked, "do you even care who killed Katherine?"

"I have a business to run, me," Baptiste said. "If you don't want a drink, you have to leave."

Clint reckoned that was the only answer he was going to get, so he turned and left.

He didn't really have any information to give Inspector Devlin, so there was no use in going to see him again.

Now he had to decide if it would be worth it to take a ride to Baton Rouge. Without any names he would have to ask around, see if anyone knew Kit Devereaux.

But before leaving for Baton Rouge, he got another idea.

When he got back to his hotel, he asked the desk clerk to get Tate for him.

"Mr. Adams," Tate said, looking apprehensive. "What can I do for you?"

"Tate, what did you do with Miss Devereaux's belongings when you emptied that room?"

"We have them in storage."

"May I see them?"

"Of course," Tate said. "Come with me."

Clint followed Tate down a hallway to a closed door, which the manager opened with a key.

"Right there, in that box," Tate said, pointing. "There wasn't much. What are you hoping to find?"

"I honestly don't know," Clint said. "Maybe I'll know when I find it."

"Well, I'll leave you to it, then," Tate said. "Help yourself to anything you think might be, uh, helpful to you."

"Thank you, Tate," Clint said.

THIRTY-SEVEN

Clint realized Tate was right. There wasn't much there. Her guns, some clothing—less than you'd think a woman like Kit would have. He didn't see any jewelry in the box. He was going to have to talk with Tate about that. There was no way Kit didn't have any jewelry, so somebody had been in the box since her death, either Tate or a desk clerk or perhaps a maid.

He was about to quit when he saw something white at the bottom of the box. He reached down and pulled out an envelope. Somebody had written her a letter, and it had come from Baton Rouge.

He put the letter in his pocket, resolving to read it when he got outside in the light. All he had in there was some light from a small window.

He left the room, pulled the door closed, and went in search of Tate again.

He found Tate's office by memory and opened the door without knocking. Tate looked up from his desk, but there was no surprise there.

"Uh, Mr. Adams—"

"I think you know what I'm going to say, Tate," Clint said, cutting him off.

"Well, uh, no—"

"I don't know who helped themselves to her jewelry, but I want it back in that box by this afternoon. If it's not there, I'm going to be very upset."

"I really couldn't tell you—"

"You have a lot of people working here," Clint said, "but I'm holding you personally responsible for the return of that jewelry!"

"That's not fair—"

Clint turned and cut the man off by leaving the office.

Back in his room he sat down and took the envelope from his pocket. He took the letter out, smoothed it. It was one page, a cramped handwriting and, judging from the signature, it was from a woman. The scrawled name could have been Belinda or Delilah; it was hard to tell.

It was a short letter. Belinda or Delilah was begging Kit to come back to Baton Rouge and not *"risk your life"* by staying in the Quarter. There was also a warning to *"stay away from your father, you know how he is."*

Clint folded the letter and returned it to the envelope. Maybe he didn't have to go to Baton Rouge, after all.

Over on Esplanade, Newman and DuBois were waiting for Dave Kendrick to arrive with his replacement.

"You think Kendrick could've taken Adams?" DuBois asked.

"I don't know," Newman said, "but we don't have to worry about that now."

"You think Cory or his partner will realize we backed their pathetic contest just to lure Adams here so we could have him killed?"

"I don't think either of them knows their contest is pathetic," Newman said. "They're both idiots."

At that point Kendrick came in with another man behind him. The man was tall, not well dressed, wearing a Colt in a worn-looking holster. As they approached the table, the second man looked bored.

"Gents," Kendrick said, "meet Willie Cain. Willie, this is Mr. Newman and that's Mr. DuBois."

"DuBois," Cain said. "That's a big New Orleans family, ain't it?"

"It is," Anton DuBois said.

"Thought so."

"Mr. Kendrick has explained the job?" Newman asked.

"You want the Gunsmith killed."

"Can you do it?"

"I'd do it for free," the man said, then grinned and added, "but I ain't going to."

"Don't worry," Newman said. "You'll be paid."

"Speakin' of getting' paid . . ." Kendrick said.

Newman took an envelope from his pocket and handed it to Kendrick. The gunman started to open it.

"Please," Newman said, "don't insult me by counting it now."

Kendrick hesitated, then said, "Ah, what the hell. It's probably all there."

"And now it's time for you to leave New Orleans," Newman said to Kendrick, "for good."

"Don't worry," Kendrick said. "I'm already gone."

Without a further word to anyone he turned on his heel and was gone.

"So," Cain asked, "when do you want Clint Adams killed?"

Newman stared after Kendrick and said, "As soon as you do one other job for us."

THIRTY-EIGHT

Later in the day, as Clint was leaving his hotel he came face-to-face with Inspector Devlin.

"I'm glad I found you here," Devlin said.

"What's going on?"

"First tell me where you've been since you left my office."

"I went to Baptiste's," Clint said, "and then I came here. I've been here ever since."

"And those marks on your neck?" Devlin asked. "You didn't have those in my office."

"No, I didn't," Clint said. "Those would be the work of Baptiste—and I want to talk to you about it."

"Me first," Devlin said. "You might want to come with me."

"Why?"

"We found Kendrick."

"Really? I thought he'd be out of town by now."

"That was his plan, I guess, only he didn't make it," Devlin said. "Somebody killed him first."

• • •

Kendrick was dead in his room in a run-down hotel near the river. He'd been shot twice.

"His gun is still in his holster," Clint said.

"I see that."

"Means he was probably shot by somebody he knew."

"I thought of that."

"Sorry."

"No, no," Devlin said, "that's okay. Make any comment that comes to mind. It can only help."

Clint walked around the small room. There was one window, opening onto an alley. The window and windowsill were dusty, indicating they hadn't been open in a long time.

"He had to have come though the front door," Clint said. "That means Kendrick let him in."

"Why would someone he knew kill him?"

"Same reason Kendrick would've killed me," Clint said. "Money."

"We searched the room, couldn't find anything helpful. But his bag was packed, and the desk clerk said Kendrick told him he'd be checking out."

"So he was leaving town, probably because he knew you were looking for him," Clint said. "And that means he wasn't going to do the job."

"So they killed him rather than let him go."

Clint walked over to the chest of drawers, which was leaning because it only had three legs. There was an empty white envelope on top. Clint picked it up.

"He could have gotten a payoff in this," Clint said, waving it.

"So whoever killed him took the money for themselves?" Devlin asked.

"Or," Clint said, "took the money back for their employers."

He put the envelope back on the chest.

"And you still don't think he killed Miss Devereaux?" Devlin asked.

"No, I don't."

"Do you have someone else in mind?"

"As a matter of fact, I do," Clint said. "That's what I wanted to talk to you about."

Devlin looked around the room, then said, "Let's go someplace else and talk about it."

They left the dock area, made their way back to the Quarter before Devlin pointed out a small saloon on a corner.

"It's quiet," he said. "I stop in here when I need some time to myself."

"To drink?" Clint asked.

"And think."

They entered, found the place almost empty. It was a no-frills watering hole. Clint figured it catered to a particular clientele, men like Devlin, who wanted to stay away from the action.

"Beer?" Devlin asked.

"Sure."

"Grab a table."

They were all empty, so Clint had his pick and took one in the back of the room. He wondered how many tables he'd sat at during his lifetime, with his back to the wall.

Devlin came over with two frothy beer mugs and put one in front of Clint. He sat across from Clint and took a grateful swallow of beer.

"Now," he said, putting his mug down, "suppose you tell me what's on your mind."

THIRTY-NINE

"Are you sure about this?" Devlin asked after listening for a few moments.

"No, I'm not," Clint said. "That's why I'm talking to you about it."

"I find it hard to believe."

"Why not? Worse things have happened."

Devlin sat back and scratched his nose.

"I must be a little naïve," he said. "This sounds about as bad as something can be."

"Look," Clint said, "I was thinking about acting on it myself, since you need evidence before you can do anything."

"If you get me some evidence," Devlin said, "I'll be there with you."

"Okay," Clint said, "what about the description of the two men I gave you?"

"Sorry," Devlin said. "There are too many dandies and gentlemen in this town for me to identify two of them from your description."

"That's okay," Clint said. "I have an idea about that, too."

"You've got lots of ideas," Devlin said.

"I know," Clint said, "but you need evidence." Clint stood up. "I'll do my best to get you some."

"I'm going to sit here awhile and finish my beer," Devlin said. "But you know where to find me."

"Yeah," Clint said. "I know."

Clint pounded on the front door of Antoine's, which was not open yet. An annoyed-looking man came to the door and Clint recognized him as the maître d'. He waved and pointed to the closed sign. Clint drew his gun and pointed through the glass with it. It was just easier than trying to explain.

The man unlocked the door.

"I'm sorry, sir, but we're—"

"I know, I know," Clint said, "you're closed. I just have some questions."

"Questions? About what?"

"I was here last night for supper."

"Were you?"

"I was with the blond woman with the—"

"Oh, yes, of course," the man said. "I remember. But . . . how can I help you?"

"There were two men also here, they left just before we did. Two well-dressed men—"

"We have many well-dressed people dining here, sir," the man said. His tone added that Clint was not one of them.

"They were being served by the same waiter who served us," Clint said. "Is he here?"

"That would be Paul, sir, and yes, he's here. Please wait."

The man closed the door but didn't lock it, so Clint assumed that he was actually going to return with the waiter, which he did.

"Sir?" Paul asked.

"Do you remember waiting on me last night?"

"Well, sir, I wait on a lot of—"

"I was with the blond woman with the big—"

"Oh, yes, sir," the waiter said, his eyes lighting up. "What can I do for you?"

"You were also waiting on two well-dressed gents on the other side of the room. Do you remember them?"

"Yes, sir."

"You do? Good. Who are they?"

"Sir?"

"I want their names."

"Well, sir—"

"You know their names," Clint said to him, even though he wasn't sure he was right.

The waiter hesitated.

"Paul," Clint said, "we can do this the easy way or the hard way."

"The easy way, sir."

"Then just tell me what I want to know."

"Yes, sir," Paul said. "I only know one of them, a gentleman named Anton DuBois—of the Garden District DuBois's."

"That means nothing to me."

"Well, they're a very prominent New Orleans family. And Anton, he's the oldest son."

"I see. Where do I find them?"

"In the Garden District, sir," Paul said. "I don't know the exact house, but the address should not be hard for you to find out."

"You're right about that," Clint said. "Thank you, Paul."

"Yes, sir."

"Tell your boss I'm sorry if I scared him."

"You did frighten him, sir," Paul said, "and for that I am grateful."

FORTY

Clint had not taken Eclipse out of the livery since his arrival in New Orleans, and he didn't do it now. Instead, he took the streetcar to the Garden District, after having retrieved the address from the morgue of the *New Orleans Picayune*. The addresses of prominent members of society were pretty much common knowledge.

Clint walked up to the door of the two-story brick house and knocked. He was about to knock a second time when the door was opened by a middle-aged black woman wearing a maid's dress.

"Suh?"

"I'd like to see Mr. Anton DuBois, please."

"Mistuh Anton?"

"That's right."

She looked confused. Before Clint could say anything else, a voice came from behind the maid.

"Who is it, Regina?"

"It's a man, ma'am," the maid replied. "He say he wanna talk to Mr. Anton."

An elegant white-haired woman appeared behind the maid.

"I'll handle this, Regina," she said. "Thank you."

"Yes, ma'am."

The older woman took the maid's place in the doorway. Clint could see that in her youth she had been a beauty, but she was at least sixty now—a well-preserved sixty.

"What is your name?"

"Clint Adams, ma'am."

"My name is Lavinia DuBois. Do I understand that you wish to speak to my son, Anton?"

"Yes, ma'am," Clint said. "Is that so hard to believe?"

"Well, frankly, yes, it is."

"But why?"

"My son is . . . well, a wastrel. You seem to be an intelligent young man."

"Well, thank you."

"So I can't understand what you could want with my son. Does he owe you money? Is that it?"

"Ma'am," Clint said, "I believe your son has hired someone to kill me."

"To kill you? That's prep— What did you say your name was?"

"Clint Adams."

"Clint—wait." Her eyes widened. "Are you the man they call the Gunsmith?"

"That's right."

"Mr. Adams," she said, "I think you had better come in."

She backed out of the doorway and Clint stepped inside.

• • •

She took Clint to a glass-enclosed area she called a solar-
ium. Without offering him any refreshment—a curious
lack of Southern hospitality—she launched into what she
thought was an explanation for her son's actions.

"Have you ever met a man named Maurice DuBois,
Mr. Adams?"

"I can't say that I have," he replied, "but I've met a
lot of men over the years."

"And have you killed many men?"

"Some."

"So many that you wouldn't recall their names?"

"No," he said. "I'd remember."

"So, you never killed a man by that name? Perhaps
ten years ago?"

"No," Clint said, "never."

"We were told—that is, someone told Anton that his
father had been killed by the Gunsmith."

"I see," Clint said. "I suppose that does explain some
of this, but I'm telling you the truth, Mrs. DuBois. I
never killed a man by that name."

She studied him for a moment, and then said, "I believe you. You see, I have no illusions about the kind of
man my husband was. Whoever killed him must have
thought they had good cause. They had probably been
swindled by him."

"Is that what he was? A swindler?"

With her arms folded she said, "That and worse."

"But . . . your family is wealthy."

"Yes, you're right," she said. "My family. Not his.
My husband was a thief and a con man. But my son is
something worse."

"What's worse?"

"I'm afraid he's . . . nothing. In fact, Anton has never done anything in his life—anything constructive or useful."

"Well, he's done something now," Clint said. "He and his friend have hired someone to kill me."

"His friend?"

"Another man, slightly older, looks like he has money."

"Anton has only one friend I know of. A waste, just like him."

"Then I guess I want both of them, ma'am," he said. "Are they here?"

"Here? No, no, I don't allow them here."

"Do you know where the other man lives?"

"As a matter of fact, I do. He lives in a house in Metairie."

"That's right near the Quarter, isn't it?"

"Yes."

"Do you have an address?"

"I do, somewhere. Wait here and I'll look."

Clint had a look around at the plants, all seemingly well cared for. He wondered if, with a dead husband and wastrel son, Mrs. DuBois had anything else to occupy herself with.

"Here you are," she said, returning to the room. "I've written it down for you. His name is Victor Newman and I have even less use for him than I do for my son."

"I understand. Thank you, Mrs. DuBois."

He started for the door, but she stopped him.

"Mr. Adams."

"Yes?"

She approached him.

"While I do believe you did not kill my husband," she said, "do you intend to kill my son?"

"No, Mrs. DuBois," he said. "But I do intend to see to it that he doesn't have me killed. To be frank, I don't know how this will turn out."

"I understand," she said.

As he left, she had already begun tending to one of her plants.

He didn't bother pointing out that while he was sure he'd never killed a man named Maurice DuBois, that didn't mean that he might not have killed the man while he was using an assumed name.

FORTY-ONE

Clint took the streetcar back to the French Quarter, then flagged down a passing hansom cab and gave the driver the address.

"That's outside the Quarter," the driver said, "in Metairie."

"I know."

The driver shrugged.

"Nothin' goin' on there, sir," he said. "I could take you to some fine places in the Quarter where you could get—"

"Just take me to that address."

The driver shrugged again and snapped the reins of his horse.

The house had once been grand, but the current resident had apparently allowed it to go to seed. The window shutters were hanging askew, a couple windows were boarded. There was furniture on the porch, but it was also in disrepair. The walkway leading to the front steps was cracked and pitted.

Clint reached the door and knocked, but instinctively knew that the house was empty. He could just feel it.

"They ain't there."

The voice came from behind him. He turned and faced three men, all armed and standing as if they knew how to use their guns.

The spokesman was the man in the center.

"I see they replaced Kendrick with three men," he said.

"Kendrick became a liability," the man in the center said. "My name's Cain, Willie Cain. These are my . . . associates."

"Where are DuBois and Newman?" Clint asked.

"Little saloon they favor over on Esplanade, near the Quarter," Cain said. "They're waitin' there to give me my money."

"After you kill me."

"Right."

"Or, at least, that's the plan."

The man smiled and said, "My plans always come together."

"You boys should step away," Clint said, "let the big man handle this himself."

The two men looked at each other.

"That way," Clint added, "only one of you will die today."

"They're gettin' paid, just like me," Cain said.

"Oh, I doubt they're getting as much money as you are, Mr. Cain."

"That's enough talkin'," Cain said. "It's time to die."

Cain's hand went for his gun. The other men obviously had instructions not to draw until he did, so they were well behind him. Clint had time to draw and fire once, hitting Cain dead center, driving all the air out of his lungs with an audible *whoosh*.

Quickly, Clint fired one shot at each of the other men. One he took high in the chest, but the other one took the bullet square in the stomach.

Clint stepped down from the porch, ejecting spent shells and replacing them with live ones. He walked past the fallen men, giving them each only a cursory glance to be sure they were dead.

Now all he knew was that the men he wanted were in a saloon on Esplanade. He figured he had to search from Decatur to N. Rampart, about seven blocks.

Surely he'd have them by late afternoon.

FORTY-TWO

Clint knew he had the right place when he got to the corner of N. Rampart. For one thing, it was the last place he had left to look in. More important, the place was run-down and on a par with the house in Metairie. It was exactly where someone like Victor Newman would choose to meet and hire a killer.

When Clint entered, he spotted the two men immediately. The younger one—no doubt Anton DuBois—saw him and started to get up, but the older man—Newman—put his hand on DuBois's arm to stop him.

Clint stopped in front of their table.

"Your killer is dead, gents," he said. "He's not coming."

"I don't know what you're talking about, Adams," Newman said.

Clint smiled.

"That lie would work better if you didn't know my name, Newman."

But the man had already realized his mistake.

"And you," Clint said, looking at DuBois, "your mother is very disappointed in you."

"You killed my father, you bastard!" DuBois said.

"I didn't even know your father, Anton," Clint said, "but from what your mother tells me, neither did you."

"His father was a con man, but he won't accept that," Newman said.

"My father was a great man—"

"Oh, shut up, Anton," Newman said. "It's all over."

"You said you believed me, Victor," DuBois said, staring at Newman. "You said if I paid you, you'd help me kill the Gunsmith."

"Anton—"

"It was his idea for me to back the shooting contest for those two buffoons," DuBois said. "I put up the money for everything! But he picked out the killers. First Kendrick, and then Cain."

"Shut up, you idiot!" Newman said. "You're giving him everything he wants."

"You boys have given me almost everything I want," Clint said.

At that point Inspector Devlin came in with some uniformed policemen.

"Mr. DuBois, Mr. Newman," he said, "you are under arrest. Take them."

As the policemen led them away, the two men were still bickering.

"Well," Devlin said, "that takes care of your problem, but what about mine?"

"That's next," Clint said. "Come on."

They entered Baptiste's, found only a few customers sitting at tables. Nobody was at the bar.

Baptiste saw them and waited with a towel over his shoulder, his massive arms folded in front of him.

"Now you both come," the black man said. "I got work to do, me. I don't have time to talk."

"Last time I was here, Baptiste," Clint said, "I almost had to shoot you to keep you from killing me."

"You come to arrest me for that?" Baptiste asked Devlin.

"No," Clint said, answering for the policeman, "he's come to arrest you for killing your own daughter."

"You talk crazy," Baptiste said.

"No, Baptiste," Clint said, "crazy is a word I would apply to you, not me. When you lose your temper, I think you go crazy. I think that's what happened with Katherine, and probably what happened with your wife."

Baptiste's eyes narrowed. He dropped his hands to his sides. Clint did not know what kind of weapon the man might have behind the bar, so he was ready, his own gun hand dangling at his side.

"What do you have to say to that, Baptiste?" Devlin asked. "I can see the marks you left on Clint's neck."

"So?" the man said. "You find marks on her neck, too?"

"No," Devlin said, "but I checked with the doctor, and she did have bruises on her arms. He said they were made by someone with big hands."

Baptiste clenched and unclenched his big hands.

"I think you better come with me, Baptiste," Devlin said.

Baptiste's eyes flicked down to something behind the bar.

"I don't know what you have beneath the bar, Baptiste," Clint said. "A club, a knife, maybe a gun, but I'd shoot you dead before you could get it out."

Baptiste glared at Clint with narrowed eyes, the whites looking almost yellow.

"She was a whore, like her mother," Baptiste said. "I go to talk to her, but she won't talk to me. She hated me, talk to me like no daughter should talk to her husband. So I killed her."

When he said "husband" instead of "father" Clint knew the man was talking about his wife, whom he had no doubt killed years ago. He was getting the two women mixed up.

Devlin took out his gun and said, "Come out from behind the bar, Baptiste, and come with me."

For a moment Clint thought Baptiste was going to go for whatever weapon he had back there, but in the end his shoulders slumped and he came out from behind the bar.

"Thanks, Adams," Devlin said. "Will you be around much longer?"

"No," Clint said, "suddenly I have very little taste for the French Quarter. I'll be leaving in the morning."

"Well, check in with me if you ever come back."

Devlin marched Baptiste outside. Clint thought about Kasey. He didn't particularly care what was happening out at the Fairgrounds with the contest, and he certainly didn't want to see either Cole Weston or Ed Cory again. As for Texas Jack Vermillion, he knew they'd cross paths again in the future. So all he needed was one more night with Kasey, and then he'd be done with New Orleans for quite some time to come.

Watch for

A DAUGHTER'S REVENGE

323rd novel in the exciting GUNSMITH series
from Jove

Coming in November!

And don't miss

THE MARSHAL FROM PARIS

The Gunsmith Giant Edition 2008

Available from Jove in November!

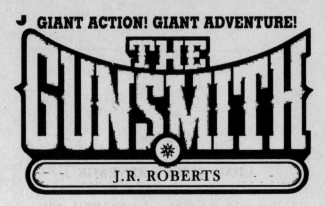

GIANT ACTION! GIANT ADVENTURE!

THE GUNSMITH

J.R. ROBERTS

penguin.com

M228AS0608

DON'T MISS A YEAR OF

Slocum Giant
by
Jake Logan

penguin.com

GIANT-SIZED ADVENTURE FROM
AVENGING ANGEL LONGARM.

BY TABOR EVANS

2006 Giant Edition:

LONGARM AND THE
OUTLAW EMPRESS

2007 Giant Edition:

LONGARM AND THE
GOLDEN EAGLE SHOOT-OUT

2008 Giant Edition:

LONGARM AND THE
VALLEY OF SKULLS

penguin.com

M240AS0508